SPIDER-MAN
THE COSMIC ADVENTURES

SPIDER-MAN®: THE COSMIC ADVENTURES
Originally published in magazine form as The Spectacular Spider-Man #'s 158, 159, 160; Web of Spider-Man #'s 59, 60, 61 and The Amazing Spider-Man #'s 327, 328, 329. Published by Marvel Comics, 387 Park Avenue South, New York, NY 10016. Copyright © 1989, 1990, 1993 Marvel Entertainment Group, Inc. All Rights Reserved. SPIDER-MAN and all prominent characters appearing herein and the distinctive names and likenesses thereof are trademarks of Marvel Entertainment Group, Inc. No part of this book may be printed or reproduced in any manner without the written permission of the publisher. Printed in The United States of America. First Printing: January, 1993. ISBN #0-87135-963-4 GST #127032852
10 9 8 7 6 5 4 3 2 1

WRITERS
Gerry Conway
chapters: 1,2,4,5,7,8

David Michelinie
chapters: 3,6,9

PENCILERS
Sal Buscema
chapters: 1,4,7

Alex Saviuk
chapers: 2,5,8

Erik Larsen
chapers: 3,9

Todd McFarlane
chapter: 6

INKERS
Mike Esposito
chapters:1,4

Keith Williams
chapters: 2,5,8

Al Gordon
chapter: 3

Todd McFarlane
chapter: 6

Sal Buscema
chapter: 7

Andy Mushynsky
chapter: 9

COLORIST
Bob Sharen

LETTERER
Rick Parker

RON LIM

pencils—front cover

KEITH WILLIAMS

inker—front cover

PAUL MOUNTS

colorist—front cover

PETER SANDERSON

introduction/afterword

DAWN GEIGER

designer

JIM SALICRUP

original series editor

ERIC FEIN

editor—reprint collection

DANNY FINGEROTH

group editor

TOM DeFALCO

editor in chief

CHRISTINE SLUSARZ

manufacturing coordinator

WITH GREATER POWER...

by Peter Sanderson

When Spider-Man first appeared in comics over thirty years ago, one of the elements that made him stand out from the other super heroes of that time was the fact that, compared to many of them, he wasn't all that "super." Sure, he had the "proportionate strength of a spider" and could lift, say, an automobile. And while he was stronger than any ordinary crook, he had plenty of adversaries who matched or exceeded his super-strength: Doctor Octopus, the Sandman, The Lizard and the Hulk just to name a few!

But the limits on Spider-Man's powers helped make him uniquely appealing. In a world where super-powered titans clashed, Spider-Man was the little guy fighting against superior odds. Thus, it was easier for readers to identify and sympathize with him.

Spider-Man was once an introverted bookworm who turned arrogant and egotistical, using his powers to seek fame and fortune. As followers of Spider-Man's history know, only when a burglar Spider-Man had allowed to go free killed his uncle Ben did Spider-Man finally realize the truth that has since guided his life--"with great power must come great responsibility."

The limitations on those powers helped keep Spider-Man humble. But what would happen if Spider-Man suddenly became even more powerful than he could ever imagine? What if suddenly, somehow, he found himself with powers that put him in the same league as the Silver Surfer, capable of flying or performing virtually any cosmic feat?

These are the questions raised by the "Cosmic Spider-Man" stories collected for the first time in this volume. They took place at a particularly eventful time in the lives of Spider-Man and his fellow super heroes, and for you to appreciate these stories fully, we must first set the scene. So take out your scorecards and get ready...

It began when a mysterious individual contacted six of the most dangerous men on Earth. There were Doctor Doom and the Wizard, who were leading enemies of the Fantastic Four but also had scores to settle with Spider-Man. There were Captain America's arch-enemy the Red Skull and Iron Man's nemesis the Mandarin. There was also the mutant Magneto, who had in recent times become the ally of his former foes the X-Men. But Magneto had just deposed Sebastian Shaw as leader of the Hellfire Club's Inner Circle, a cabal seeking world domination. Finally, there was Wilson Fisk, the Kingpin of Crime, then still the absolute master of New York's organized crime and the bitter, longtime enemy of Spider-Man.

The stranger's plan was simple. He proposed that these six criminal masterminds organize an all-out assault against the super heroes, pitting them against super-villains they had never fought before and with whom therefore they wouldn't be familiar. Thus began the war of the super-villains against the super heroes that became known as the "Acts of Vengeance."

It was a miracle that Spider-Man survived the first assault in the "Acts of Vengeance." The Kingpin enlisted Graviton, one of the Avengers' most dangerous foes who had gained the power to control the force of gravity. Seeking to lure Spider-Man into his grasp, Graviton effortlessly levitated the Daily Bugle building into the air!

The one man most associated with the Bugle, however, publisher J. Jonah Jameson, was not present. Spider-Man's sometime adversary, the Puma, alias businessman Thomas Fireheart, believed he owed Spider-Man a debt of honor, for as the Puma he had attacked Spider-Man, thinking the web-spinner had committed a crime. Knowing that Jameson was constantly attacking Spider-Man through his Bugle editorials, Fireheart tried to settle his debt of honor by buying the Bugle out from under Jameson and using it instead to *promote* Spider-Man's reputation.

Spider-Man put up a brave fight against Graviton, but was soundly defeated. He wasn't powerful enough. But soon he would find himself with all the power he could ever have dreamed of and more!

Read on...and enjoy!

CHAPTER 1

ONE MINUTE AGO, LIFE WAS GOOD.

THE SUN WAS SHINING OVER THE EAST SIDE OF MANHATTAN, AND SOMEWHERE IN QUEENS, A BIRD WAS CHIRPING WITH MERRY DELIGHT.

YES, ONE MINUTE AGO, HE WAS A FRIENDLY NEIGHBORHOOD SPIDER-MAN ON HIS WAY TO MEET HIS LOVELY BRIDE FOR AN EARLY DINNER IN THEIR FAVORITE SOUTH STREET SEAPORT RESTAURANT.

IT JUST GOES TO SHOW HOW QUICKLY THINGS CAN CHANGE IN LESS THAN SIXTY SECONDS.

EEEEE-YUCK!

WHAT THE HECK IS THIS?!

THE PASTE AND THE POWER

(OR A VERY STICKY SITUATION)

"-- MAYBE *MORE* SO, SINCE I CAN SHOOT PASTE OR GREASE OR EVEN *EXPLODING GUMBALLS* -- "

≥YUNNGH≤ THIS IS *DISGUSTING!*

"-- WHILE ALL *YOU* CAN DO IS FIRE A FEW *WEBS!*"

WAITAMINUTE! PASTE! GREASE! GUM-BALLS!

I KNOW YOU! YOU'RE THE GUY THE HUMAN TORCH USED TO CALL *PASTE-POT PETE!*

THAT'S *ANCIENT HISTORY,* SPIDER-MAN!

FOR A LONG TIME NOW, I'VE BEEN *THE TRAPSTER..*

"-- AND I THINK YOU JUST FOUND OUT *WHY!*"

GREASE-- UNDER MY *FEET!*

CAN'T-- HANG--

--OONNNZZZN!

SEE WHAT I MEAN?

I SET THE *TRAP*-- GOT YOU ALL *DISORIENTED..* AND YOU FELL RIGHT *INTO* IT!

SO TO *SPEAK.*

HAHAHA

9

I **DID** IT!

DR. OCTOPUS COULDN'T DO IT, *THE VULTURE* NEVER HAD A CHANCE --

-- ELECTRO, MYSTERIO *HOBGOBLIN* AND *PUMA* --

-- ALL OF THEM *WIMPS*!

WHEN PUSH CAME TO SHOVE, ONLY *ONE* GUY HAD WHAT IT TOOK TO *WASTE* THE WEBSLINGER!

ME! *THE TRAPSTER!*

MAYBE *NOW* PEOPLE WON'T BE SO QUICK TO CALL ME "PASTE-POT PETE!"

HA!

UH... MJ... HE'S BEEN DOWN THERE A PRETTY *LONG TIME*, HASN'T HE?

YOU THINK HE'S--?

NO!

HE'S ALIVE -- ANY SECOND NOW, HE'LL JUMP TO THE *SURFACE!*

YOU'LL SEE...

YOU'LL SEE...

OH, PETER --! PLEASE DON'T MAKE ME A LIAR! I'LL NEVER *FORGIVE* YOU!

SP0OSH

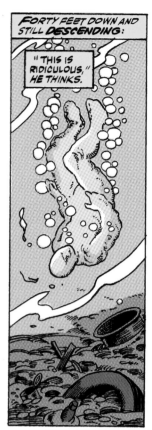

FORTY FEET DOWN AND STILL *DESCENDING:*

"THIS IS RIDICULOUS," HE THINKS.

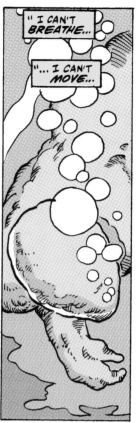

"I CAN'T *BREATHE...*

"...I CAN'T *MOVE...*

"...I'VE GOT AN ITCH ON MY NOSE I CAN'T *SCRATCH...*

"...I CAN'T EVEN *SEE.*

"REMINDS ME OF THE *TUXEDO* I WORE THE DAY MJ AND I GOT MARRIED.

"MJ.

"SHE HAS TO BE WORRIED *SICK.*

"OKAY, WEB-SLINGER... *DO* SOMETHING.

"AND DO IT *NOW--*

"--OR SOMEDAY THEY'LL DREDGE YOU FROM THIS RIVER AS PART OF A FRESHWATER *RECLAMATION* PROJECT!

"*DO IT, PETER!*

"*DO IT!*

WOOM

GASP!

ALL RIGHT!

HE'S OKAY, MARY JANE!

WHAT A GUY! WHAT AN INSPIRATION!

I'M GOING TO CALL MY *AGENT!* IF SPIDER-MAN CAN BEAT THE ODDS LIKE THAT, WHEN IT'S *LIFE* AND *DEATH*--

-- *I* CAN BEAT THE ODDS WITH MY *ACTING CAREER*--

BEAT THE ODDS ON YOUR *OWN* TIME, STEPH. RIGHT NOW, I WANT YOU TO BUS UP THIS MESS-- *PRONTO.*

OH... YESSIR, MR. BOSS, SIR.

¿WHEW!¿ I NEVER THOUGHT NEW YORK SMOG COULD SMELL SO *GOOD!*

THERE'S MJ-- LOOKING AS *RELIEVED* AS I FEEL.

I'LL HEAD HOME...

"...AND JUDGING BY THE *LOOK* SHE'S GIVING ME, SHE'LL BE RIGHT ON MY HEELS."

FORGET LUNCH, STEPHAN.

BUT THANKS FOR THE GREAT SERVICE ...SEE YOU ANOTHER TIME, WHEN PETER AND I CAN STAY FOR *LUNCH.*

HUH? OH, SURE, MJ.

AND BY THE WAY-- YOU *CAN* BEAT THE ODDS.

A *FIVE DOLLAR TIP* ON A ONE DOLLAR CUP OF COFFEE?

SHEEEE...

...WITH FRIENDS LIKE MARY JANE WATSON-PARKER ON MY SIDE, MAYBE I *CAN* BEAT THE ODDS AFTER ALL!

A *FIVE* BUCK TIP ON A *FOUR* BUCK RIDE?

WHADDAYOU, LADY-- *RICH?*

NOT RICH...

--JUST GRATEFUL MY MAN IS *ALIVE*--

--EVEN IF HE *DID* LEAVE A PASTY MESS ACROSS OUR NEW LOFT'S FLOOR.

WE'VE BEEN SO WORRIED ABOUT *FINANCES* LATELY--UNTIL I LANDED THAT JOB ACTING IN A T.V. *SOAP OPERA*--

--WE'D ALMOST *FORGOTTEN* WHAT REALLY MATTERS IN LIFE:

THE PEOPLE YOU *LOVE*...

PETER?

HI, HON.

SORRY ABOUT THE FLOOR...

OH, FORGET THE FLOOR.

HOW ARE *YOU?*

SOGGY... SORE... AND PRETTY *EMBARRASSED.*

HE *BEAT* ME, M.J.

ALL HE HAD WAS PASTE AND GREASE--AND HE *BEAT* ME. I DON'T KNOW WHICH IS *WORSE*...

...THE ANXIETY OF ALMOST BEING *KILLED*...

...OR THE *HUMILIATION* OF LOSING TO SUCH A *LOSER*.

GIVE YOURSELF A BREAK. YOU'RE *ALIVE*.

TO ME, THAT'S ALL THAT COUNTS.

BUT WHY DID THE TRAPSTER *ATTACK* ME IN THE FIRST PLACE? I HARDLY *KNOW* THE CREEP.

I WISH I DIDN'T HAVE TO HELP PROFESSOR LUBISCH WITH HIS EXPERIMENTS AT *EMPIRE UNIVERSITY* THIS AFTERNOON.

IT'S JUST A HUNCH, BUT I HAVE A FEELING SOMETHING PRETTY *STRANGE* IS GOING ON...

TO FIND OUT *HOW STRANGE*, LET'S LOOK *ELSEWHERE* IN MANHATTAN;

SPECIFICALLY, THE MIDTOWN OFFICE TOWER OWNED BY WILSON FISK...

...a.k.a. *THE KINGPIN OF CRIME.*

YOU *INSULT* ME, SIR.

YOU COME HERE WITHOUT INVITATION OR INTRODUCTION--

--AND TELL ME I'VE *MISMANAGED* MY CAMPAIGNS AGAINST *SPIDER-MAN* AND *DAREDEVIL.*

YOU THEN HAVE THE AUTHORITY TO OFFER YOUR SERVICES AS A *"POWER BROKER"* BETWEEN ME AND OTHERS *"IN MY SITUATION,"*

I HAVE ONLY TWO QUESTIONS FOR YOU, SIR: WHAT PRECISELY IS A *"POWER BROKER"*--

--AND WHY SHOULD I ALLOW YOU TO LEAVE MY OFFICE *ALIVE*?

RATHER THAN ANSWER YOUR QUESTIONS WITH AN *EXPLANATION*--

-- I PREFER TO PROVIDE A *DEMONSTRATION* OF WHAT MY EMPLOYERS PROPOSE.

OBSERVE.

STEP THROUGH THAT DOOR, KINGPIN -- -- AND JOIN THE OTHER CORE MEMBERS OF OUR ENTERPRISE.

WHAT IS THIS, A TELEPORTATION DEVICE?

OF A SORT.

EACH DOOR IN THIS CHAMBER OPENS TO THE PRIVATE HEADQUARTERS OF A DIFFERENT CORE LEADER.

YOU ARE THE FOURTH TO JOIN US...

I KNOW THESE MEN, THE WIZARD, DR. DOOM, MAGNETO...

AND WHO'S ON THAT TELEVISION SCREEN? PASTE POT PETE?

THE TRAPSTER, BLAST IT.

I WAS JUST REPORTING TO YOUR PALS, KINGPIN --

SPIDER-MAN IS DEAD, I KILLED HIM!

ASTOUNDING, IT WOULD APPEAR OUR THEORY IS CORRECT:

BY TRADING ENEMIES, WE HAVE FOUND A SURE PATH TO VENGEANCE AGAINST OUR LONG-TERM FOES.

IT MAKES SENSE, DOOM.

OVER THE YEARS, IN BATTLE AFTER BATTLE, OUR PERSONAL ENEMIES HAVE LEARNED OUR STRATEGIES AND TECHNIQUES.

THEY KNOW HOW TO COUNTER OUR ATTACKS ALMOST INSTINCTIVELY.

BUT BY SWITCHING FOES -- WE REGAIN THE ADVANTAGE OF SURPRISE.

VENGEANCE IS OURS-- BY PROXY.

YOU SAY THIS BUFFOON SUCCEEDED AT DESTROYING SPIDER-MAN WHERE I FAILED?

I WON'T BELIEVE IT UNTIL I'VE SEEN THE BODY.

YOU WANT PROOF I'LL GET PROOF.

THEN IT'S YOUR TURN TO WASTE MY ENEMIES, FAT MAN.

LET'S SEE HOW YOU DO AGAINST THE HUMAN TORCH!

AHEM. KNOWING YOU WERE COMING, KINGPIN, WE ARRANGED SPIDER-MAN'S DEATH AS A PREMIUM.

BUT THERE ARE CERTAIN QUID PRO QUOS INVOLVED IN THESE ACTS OF VENGEANCE...

QUITE SO.

A DEATH FOR A DEATH.

AN ENEMY FOR AN ENEMY.

MONDAY AFTERNOON. EMPIRE STATE UNIVERSITY. THE PHYSICS LAB OF PROFESSOR MAX LUBISCH.

OH, YES, OH YES, THIS WILL BE WONDERFUL!

MAYBE SO...

...IF WE DON'T OVERLOAD THE UNIVERSITY POWER LINES AND BLOW THE WHOLE CON EDISON POWER GRID FOR LOWER MANHATTAN.

PROFESSOR, EXCUSE ME FOR ASKING-- DID YOU HAVE THE ENGINEERING DEPARTMENT CHECK THE SPECIFICATIONS FOR THIS MACHINE?

NO NEED, PETER. I CHECKED THEM MYSELF.

UH-HUH. WHEN YOU ASKED PROFESSOR SWANN IF YOU COULD BORROW ME TO ASSIST YOU ON THIS EXPERIMENT--

--YOU SAID YOU WANTED TO TAP A PREVIOUSLY "UNKNOWN ENERGY SOURCE,".

WOULDN'T THE ENGINEERING DEPARTMENT BE--

NONSENSE. IN MY HOMELAND I BUILT MANY MACHINES.

ONLY A FEW EVER MALFUNCTIONED WHILE-- LOOK!

IT'S WORKING!

WE'VE LOCKED INTO AN EXTRA-DIMENSIONAL ENERGY SOURCE -- JUST AS I PREDICTED!

MAYBE SO -- MAYBE NOT -- BUT JUST AS I PREDICTED--

"-- THIS MACHINE IS OVERLOADING THE UNIVERSITY ELECTRICAL SYSTEM!

"IT ISN'T OUT OF CONTROL, NOT YET-- BUT JUDGING BY THE WAY STATIC ELECTRICITY IS BUILDING UP AROUND THIS ROOM--!

WHEW. AND DOUBLE WHEW. WHATEVER HIT ME-- AND GRAZED THE PROFESSOR-- PROBABLY WOULD HAVE KILLED HIM--

--OR ANYONE ELSE WITHOUT A SPIDER-ENHANCED METABOLISM LIKE MINE TO PROTECT HIM.

EVEN SO, I FEEL LIKE I JUST SWALLOWED A FRESH CAR BATTERY.

MY STOMACH TINGLES, AND MY MOUTH TASTES LIKE ACID AND METAL.

MAYBE I BETTER SIT DOWN A MOMENT UNTIL I --

OWWW.!

SPIDER-SENSE-- CLANGING LIKE A THREE-ALARM FIRE! NEVER FELT IT SO INTENSELY BEFORE!

DANGER OUTSIDE-- THE POWER LINES-- SHORTING OUT-- THREATENING THOSE STUDENTS ON THE CAMPUS QUAD--!

PROFESSOR LUBISCH IS ALREADY COMING AROUND, SO I CAN LEAVE HIM...

...AND TAKE CARE OF THIS SIDE-EFFECT OF TODAY'S LITTLE "EXPERIMENT" AS SPIDER-MAN.

≥GROAN≤ PAINFUL... VERY PAINFUL, OH, YES... BUT WE WERE SUCCESSFUL, OH, YES...

... VERY SUCCESSFUL... AND ONE CANNOT DO SCIENCE WITHOUT A LITTLE PAIN, PETER... OH YES...

eh?

OH, MY...

WHY IS LIFE NEVER EASY? BROKEN POWER LINES FLIPPING AROUND LIKE HUNGRY EELS!

GOTTA *CATCH* 'EM BEFORE THOSE *KIDS* ON THE QUAD GET--

OHMIGOD!

INCREDIBLE...

IMPOSSIBLE...

THAT LIVE WIRE--YOU SAW IT *SPARKING!*

IT COULD HAVE HIT US--WE COULD'VE BEEN *KILLED*-- BUT HE-- H-HE--

Y-YEAH...

H-HOW DID HE *DO* THAT?

I SHOULD BE DEAD.

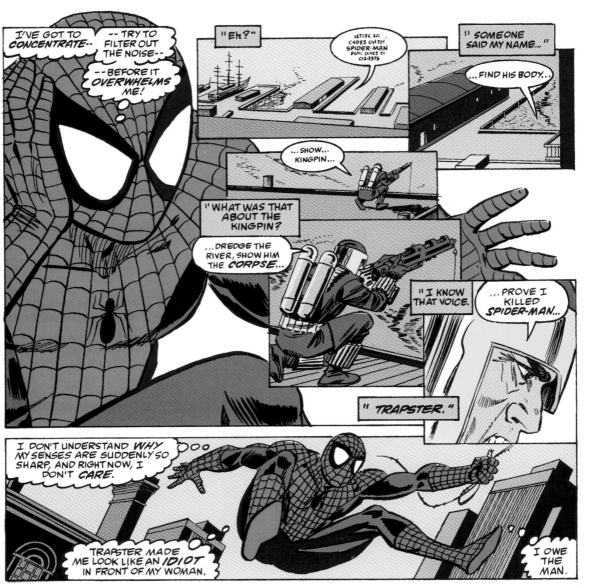

WORD OF *ADVICE*. A GUY WHO NEEDS AS MUCH *DENTAL WORK* AS YOU DO SHOULDN'T STAND AROUND WITH HIS *MOUTH* OPEN THAT WAY.

WOW!

LOOK, EVERYBODY-- *SPIDER-MAN'S* BACK! I THINK HE JUST CHALLENGED TRAPSTER TO A *REMATCH!*

I THOUGHT I *KILLED* YOU.

SO I WAS *OFF* BY A FEW HOURS.

BEEP

SUITS ME. NOW I WON'T WASTE TIME FISHING FOR YOUR BODY.

" I'LL KNOW *JUST* WHERE TO FIND YOU..."

RTOOM

OH, GREAT.

VRROOMM

HA!

MY TRAPPER- MISSILE IS LOCKED ONTO YOUR *BODY TEMP SIGNATURE,* WEB-SLINGER.

YOU CAN'T *DODGE* IT--

--AND YOU SURE AS HECK CAN'T *CATCH* IT!

FINALLY GOT YOU WHERE I WANT YOU, *TRAPPED* LIKE A--

--LIKE A--

--A--

SKR CH

HEY! I DIDN'T KNOW SPIDER-MAN'S WEB COULD DO *THAT!*

-- I MEAN--

HOW DID HE *DO* THAT?

IT CAN'T! I MEAN, IT *DIDN'T*--

I-I DON'T GET IT! YOU'RE NOT SUPPOSED TO-- YOU CAN'T--YOU NEVER--

GOTTA BE A *TRICK!*

GOTTA BE A--

ZAP ZAP ZAP ZAP

BCHOOM BCHOOM BCHOOM

BCHOO

MY PASTE-PELLETS... ...YOU BLEW ALL MY PASTE-PELLETS...

MESSY ISN'T IT?

BEFORE I HAUL YOU TO THE SHOWERS AT *POLICE PLAZA*, TELL ME WHO HIRED YOU UP TO ATTACK ME? *THE KINGPIN?*

YOU'LL FIND OUT, ONE'A US WILL GET YOU.

I'M ONLY THE *SECOND*.

ONLY THE SECOND?

ONLY THE SECOND OF *WHAT?* OF *WHO?*

NOTHING, HE SAID ALL HE'S *GOING* TO SAY.

I'VE GOT A *REAL* BAD FEELING ABOUT THIS...

SPIDER-MAN, THAT WAS *OUTRAGEOUS!*

HOW'D YOU MAKE A FIST WITH YOUR *WEB?* AND THOSE *RAYS* OUTTA YOUR FINGERTIPS--

I NEVER KNEW YOU COULD DO STUFF LIKE THAT!

NEITHER DID I.

AND FRANKLY, FRIEND, IT SCARES ME *SPITLESS*...

CHAPTER 2

A FEW HOURS AGO, I WAS YOUR AVERAGE HAPPY-GO-LUCKY, FRIENDLY NEIGHBOR-HOOD *WEB-SPINNER*...

...A GUY WITH THE PROPORTIONATE STRENGTH OF A *SPIDER*, AND A FEW EXTRA ABILITIES LIKE MY EVER-POPULAR *SPIDER-SENSE.*

I HAD *POWER*, BUT I *KNEW* WHAT IT WAS, AND I KNEW HOW TO *DEAL* WITH IT.

THEN SUDDENLY, *ZAP*, EVERYTHING CHANGED-- I GOT HIT BY AN OVERLOADED *ENERGY FIELD* DURING AN EXPERIMENT AT *EMPIRE UNIVERSITY*--

-- AND NOW I'VE GOT MORE *POTENTIAL* THAN I KNOW WHAT TO DO WITH.

I'M OVER-WHELMED, MARY JANE.

I HAD TROUBLE ENOUGH BALANCING POWER AND RESPONSIBILITY WHEN I WAS JUST PLAIN OLD *SPIDER-MAN*...

...BUT *NOW*...

NOW, YOU'RE SOMETHING *MORE*.

BUT YOU'RE STILL THE SAME *WONDERFUL* MAN I LOVE.

NO MATTER *HOW* MUCH POWER YOU POSSESS, I KNOW YOU'LL DO YOUR BEST TO HANDLE IT *RESPONSIBLY.*

THANKS, MJ.

IF I NEED *ANYTHING* RIGHT NOW, IT'S YOUR VOTE OF CONFIDENCE.

STILL, UNTIL I UNDERSTAND THIS POWER-- WHERE IT CAME FROM, AND WHAT IT'S FOR-- I DON'T DARE *USE* IT.

MAYBE YOU SHOULD COME DOWNSTAIRS TO THE *APARTMENT*-- WE CAN *TALK*--

I'D LIKE THAT.

BUT PETER PARKER HAS AN APPOINTMENT WITH THE *DAILY BUGLE'S* NEW *PUBLISHER* IN TEN MINUTES, UPTOWN--

-- AND *THOMAS FIREHEART* ISN'T A MAN WHO LIKES TO BE KEPT WAITING.

THANKS FOR THE SUPPORT, HON.

I'LL SEE YOU AT HOME, LATER.

BE KIND TO YOURSELF, PETER.

YOU ALWAYS WORRY ABOUT HOW YOUR ACTIONS AND DECISIONS CAN AFFECT *OTHERS*...

"... JUST ONCE, I WISH YOU'D THINK ABOUT HOW THEY AFFECT *YOU*."

ELSEWHERE:

*I*N A DARKENED ROOM, A MAN IN AN IRON MASK LISTENS IMPASSIVELY TO THE NEAR-SILENT *GRUNTS* OF A WEIGHTLIFTER IN MID-ROUTINE.

THE MAN'S NAME IS *DR. DOOM*.

HE IS PREPARING AN *ACT* OF *VENGEANCE*.

KRASH

WHAT ARE YOU *SAYING?*

I'M NOT *GOOD* ENOUGH TO WORK WITH THE "BIG BOYS," 'CAUSE THAT GREEN-HAIRED WENCH TOOK ME DOWN WITH A *LUCKY PUNCH?*

NOT AT ALL.

EACH OF MY COLLEAGUES IN THIS INFORMAL ASSOCIATION HAS MET *DEFEAT* AT THE HANDS OF A SPECIFIC ENEMY, TITANIA.

EVEN I.

FOR DOOM, THE ENEMY I CANNOT SEEM TO BEST HAS ALWAYS BEEN *REED RICHARDS* OF THE *FANTASTIC FOUR*--

--A FOE YOU, TOO, *FAILED* TO OVERCOME, QUITE RECENTLY. *

YEAH?

SO *WHAT?*

* AS A MEMBER OF THE *FRIGHTFUL FOUR,* IN FANTASTIC FOUR 333.--JIM

SO I SUGGEST AN *ALTERNATIVE* APPROACH TO YOUR QUEST FOR VENGEANCE AGAINST *JENNIFER WALTERS,* THE SELF-STYLED SHE-HULK.

ALLOW SOMEONE *ELSE* TO DESTROY *YOUR* HATED ENEMY, SOMEONE WHOSE ATTACK WILL BE FRESH, UNSUSPECTED, AND *IRRESISTIBLE*...

...WHILE, IN RETURN, *YOU* ASSAULT A LESS-FAMILIAR OPPONENT--AGAINST WHOM YOU WILL BE EQUALLY FRESH, UNSUSPECTED, AND *IRRE-SISTIBLE.*

SP-SPIDER-MAN?

Y-YOU WANT ME TO FIGHT *SPIDER-MAN?*

NO... I... CAN'T...

YES, I'D *HEARD* THAT YOU HAVE AN *IRRATIONAL* FEAR OF THAT CURSED ARACHNID.

APPARENTLY, HE DEFEATED YOU QUITE *BADLY* SHORTLY AFTER I GAVE YOU YOUR POWERS, DURING OUR SOJOURN ON THE BEYONDER'S WORLD, SOME MONTHS AGO. *

OR *DID* HE?

D-DIDN'T HE?

*IN *SECRET WARS #7.* --J.S.

A PUNY COSTUMED *BUG* LIKE THAT?

HOW COULD HE HAVE BEAT YOU--YOU, WHO CAN LIFT *85* TONS TO HIS 10?

HOW, UNLESS--

UNLESS...?

HE *TRICKED* YOU.

ISN'T IT *OBVIOUS*?

YOU WERE NEVER BEATEN --IT WAS ALL A *TRICK*.

A TRICK!

THAT PUNY COSTUMED *BUG*!

I'LL *KILL* HIM! I'LL SQUEEZE HIM SO HARD, HIS HEAD'LL POP LIKE A *ZIT*!

BUT *HOW*? WHERE CAN I *FIND* HIM?

PROBABLY THROUGH HIS *NEW FRIENDS* AT THE *DAILY BUGLE*...

"UNSUNG HERO?"

THAT PUNY COSTUMED *BUG*?

DAILY BUGLE

SPIDER-MAN: NEW YORK'S GREATEST UNSUNG HERO

I'VE GOT YOUR UNSUNG HERO *RIGHT HERE*--!

KA-BOOM

AAARRRRHH!

32

PUNY COSTUMED BUG... PUNY COSTUMED BUG... *TRICKED* ME... POP HIM LIKE A ZIT...

WHY *WAIT* ANOTHER MOMENT?

DESTROY HIM...

...IF YOU *CAN.*

WHICH I SINCERELY *DOUBT.* ACCORDING TO MY ALLY IN THESE *ACTS OF VENGEANCE,* THE WIZARD, TITANIA'S FORMER TEAM-LEADER IN THE FRIGHT-FUL FOUR--

--TITANIA'S FEAR OF *SPIDER-MAN* SHOULD HAVE MADE HER AN UNSUITABLE WEAPON AGAINST THE WEB-SLINGER.

BUT *DOOM* IS A MASTER OF ELEC-TRONICS--

-- AND THE DEVICE I PLANTED ON HER SHOULDER WHEN I TOUCHED HER MOMENTS AGO CONVERTED HER FEAR INTO MINDLESS *RAGE.*

STILL, TITANIA'S CHANCES AGAINST *SPIDER-MAN* ARE PROBLEMATIC AT BEST.

FOR HE IS NO LONGER A MERE SPINNER OF WEBS, AS *THE TRAPSTER* DISCOVERED TO HIS MORTIFICATION.

SOMEHOW, *SPIDER-MAN* HAS CHANGED...GROWN MORE *POWERFUL.*

MORE EVEN THAN HIS DESTRUCTION, I DESIRE TO UNDER-STAND THE *NATURE* OF HIS NEW POWERS...

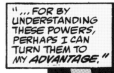

"...FOR BY UNDERSTANDING THESE POWERS, PERHAPS I CAN TURN THEM TO MY *ADVANTAGE.*"

"AFTER ALL, GREATER POWER IS THE ULTIMATE DESTINY OF *DOOM.*"

JONAH JAMESON DOESN'T OWN THE *DAILY BUGLE* ANYMORE...

...*I DO.*..

... AND FROM NOW ON, I WANT OUR PAPER TO REFLECT A DIFFERENT APPROACH TO *REPORTAGE--*

--PARTICULARLY WHEN IT COMES TO OUR COVERAGE OF *SPIDER-MAN.*

YOU ALL SAW THIS MORNING'S HEADLINE, WHICH I PERSONALLY SUGGESTED TO OUR CITY EDITOR, *KATE CUSHING.*

THE OLD NEGATIVE, MEAN-SPIRITED SPIDER-MAN BASHING PROMOTED BY YOUR FORMER PUBLISHER IS *OUT.*

A MORE BALANCED, EVEN-HANDED, POSITIVE FORM OF ADVOCACY JOURNALISM IS *IN.*

DAILY BUGLE — HERO OR MENACE?

DAILY BUGLE — OUR WEBBED HERO

BLAH-BLAH-BLAH. THESE HOTSHOT HONCHOS MAKE ME SICK.

WHOA, MAMA-- NOW THAT'S WHAT I CALL A BABE...

HEY, WATCHIT! THAT'S MY *FOOT*-- HUH?

PARKER! SHOULD'A FIGURED IT'D BE YOU.

SORRY, NICK.

YES, RIGHT. EVERY TIME I TURN AROUND, YOU'RE IN MY FACE.

AND WHAT A LOVELY FACE IT IS.

MR. FIREHEART, THIS IS *OUT-RAGEOUS.* YOU SAY YOU WANT BALANCED JOURNALISM--

--BUT YOUR "POSITIVE ADVOCACY" IS JUST AS *BIASED* AS MR. JAMESON'S ANTI-SPIDER-MAN CAMPAIGN.

REALLY, MS. CUSHING?

PERHAPS YOU HAVE A POINT. LET'S DISCUSS IT IN MY OFFICE.

WE'LL LEAVE THE REST OF YOU TO YOUR *WORK.*

WHAT A SWITCH-- HUH, PETER?

THINK KATE WILL HAVE ANY MORE LUCK SHIFTING FIREHEART'S BIASES THAN SHE HAD SHIFTING JONAH'S?

SOMEHOW, I DOUBT IT, JOY.

ASK ME, IT'S A *SELLOUT!*

FIREHEART'S GOT NO MORE JOURNALISTIC INTEGRITY THAN A-- THAN A--

THAN A *NICK KATZENBERG.*

OHO, DON'T BE SO QUICK TO *JUDGE* OUR FAVORITE FORMER SUPERMARKET TABLOID SHUTTERBUG, PETE.

WHY ALL THE PHOTOS OF *CYNTHIA BERNHAMMER,* NICK?

UH-- AH-- SHE'S THE BUGLE'S *LEGAL COUNSEL...*

...AND WHAT WITH THE *ROBBIE ROBERTSON* APPEAL GETTING SO MUCH PLAY... I FIGURE WE NEED MORE *PICS* OF THE LADY, THAT'S ALL!

TOUCHY, TOUCHY!

GIMME THAT.

TELL US, NICK-- DOES CYNTHIA-- KNOW SHE HAS A *DON JUAN* IN HER FUTURE?

CUT IT OUT, YOU GUYS. I'M *WARNING* YOU--

SOMEBODY BETTER WARN *CYNTHIA,*

THE SHOCK OF SEEING YOU WITH ROSES AT HER DOOR MIGHT JUST--

HUH? TALK ABOUT *WARNINGS--!*

MY SPIDER-SENSE IS *BUZZING* SO HARD I CAN'T--

SKTOOM!

WHERE IS HE?

WHERE IS THAT PUNY COSTUMED BUG?

OMIGOSH, THAT'S *TITANIA!* SHE USED TO HANG AROUND WITH *THE ABSORBING MAN!*

IT'S BEEN A WHILE SINCE I LAST SAW HER, BUT SIX-FOOT-SIX FEMALES ARE KIND OF HARD TO *FORGET*...

TELL ME WHERE TO *FIND* HIM-- --OR I'LL TAKE THIS PLACE APART SO *QUICK,* YOU'LL FIND YOURSELVES STANDING ON *AIR!*

SHEESH, LADY! FIND *WHO?*

SPIDER-MAN-- WHO DO YOU *THINK?*

WHAT ARE YOU ALL-- *STUPID?*

LISTEN WHEN I'M TALKING TO YOU!

DOESN'T MAKE SENSE! WHAT'S TITANIA *DOING* HERE--

--AND WHY DOES SHE WANT *ME?*

SURE, WE'VE *FOUGHT* IN THE PAST--

--BUT SHE'S NEVER BEEN ONE OF MY REAL *ENEMIES*--!

PHOT

38

HEY, *PUMA*, DIDN'T YOUR MOTHER EVER TELL YOU--

--IT ISN'T SMART TO GO FLYING WITHOUT YOUR *WINGS* ON?

THWIPP

WELL, THAT'S *ONE* WASTED WISECRACK.

I'LL BET THE ONLY THING PUMA CAN HEAR RIGHT NOW IS THE SOUND OF LITTLE *BIRDIES* FLUTTERING AROUND HIS HEAD.

LUCKY FOR HIM I MANAGED TO SLIP OUT A WINDOW IN THE *PHOTO LAB* IN TIME TO PLAY "CATCH THE FALLING CAT-MAN."

FIREHEART ALREADY THINKS HE OWES ME A "*DEBT OF HONOR*"--THAT'S WHY HE BOUGHT THE *DAILY BUGLE.*

NOW THAT I'VE SAVED HIS HIDE, I MAY *NEVER* BE DONE WITH THE GUY,

LUCKY FOR HIM, UNLUCKY FOR ME.

GREAT, *ANOTHER* PROBLEM:

THOSE "POWERS" I PICKED UP HAVE ENHANCED MY *SPIDER-SENSE* SO MUCH IT'S ON PERMANENT *OVERLOAD.*

BUZZING SO LOUD I CAN'T *THINK!*

GOTTA CLAMP DOWN-- *FORCE* MYSELF TO--

≥OWWW!≤

41

42

-- I BREAK PAVEMENT--

-- I GET PUNCHED INTO A FLAGPOLE AND SWATTED WITH SIDEWALK--

-- I FLATTEN THE HOOD OF A CAR--

--AND ALL I SAY IS "OUCH?"

WHAT'S HAPPENED TO ME?

BLAST YOU, BUG! HOW MANY TIMES DO I HAVE TO SMASH YOU?

WHY WON'T YOU DIE?

LADY, BELIEVE IT, OR NOT--

FURNITURE CO.

--I'M ASKING MYSELF THAT SAME QUESTION.

BY THE WAY, WATCH OUT BEHIND YOU.

DON'T TRY TO TRICK ME AGAIN, YOU PUNY COSTUMED BU--

--UH?

I TOLD YOU, WOMAN--

THE WEB-SPINNER IS UNDER MY PROTECTION!

EEK! I'M SO SCARED! TELL ME, FRISKY-FUR...

"PUMA'S CLAWS RIPPED MY MICRO-SENSOR/ CONTROLLER FROM TITANIA'S SHOULDER..."

WHO PROTECTS YOU?!

SWAK

RRRIP

"HOW UNFORTUNATE.

-- A PUNY COSTUMED **BUG!**

WHAM

"HMMM.

"WHAT AN *INTRIGUING* DEVELOPMENT.

"AS I'VE ALWAYS KNOWN, FEAR AND RAGE ARE BUT TWO SIDES OF A PSYCHIC COIN.

"WHEN HER RAGE WAS *LIB-ERATED* BY MY SENSOR/CONTROLLER, TITANIA CONQUERED HER FEAR,,,

",,,AND THOUGH THE FEAR *RETURNED* TO HER, BRIEFLY AFTER THE SENSOR'S *LOSS*,,,

",,,ULTIMATELY HER ANGER PROVED MORE *POWERFUL* THAN THE FEAR THAT REPLACED IT.

"WHICH RAISES THE *QUESTION* OF COURSE:

" WHEN WILL SPIDER-MAN'S ANGER OVERCOME *HIS* FEAR ?

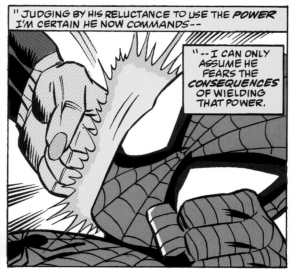

" JUDGING BY HIS RELUCTANCE TO USE THE *POWER* I'M CERTAIN HE NOW COMMANDS--

"-- I CAN ONLY ASSUME HE FEARS THE *CONSEQUENCES* OF WIELDING THAT POWER.

I DON'T BELIEVE I *DID* THAT!

AFTER ALL THE EFFORT I MADE TO KEEP MY NEW POWERS IN CHECK-- TO *ROLL* WITH THE PUNCHES, AND JUST WEAR HER DOWN--

--I *LOSE* IT LIKE A KID IN A *SCHOOLYARD!*

HUH?

SPIDER-SENSE BUZZING AGAIN-- BUT THIS TIME IT'S NOT JUST GENERAL *ANXIETY*--

--IT'S TELLING ME THERE'S *DANGER* NEARBY:

I FEEL LIKE I'M BEING *WATCHED!*

HUH? *NOW* WHAT...?

SOME KIND OF *SUPER-VISION*--

--SHOWING ME *NICK KATZENBERG* TAKING PHOTOS FROM THE BUGLE'S OFFICE THIRTY STORIES UP!

IS NICK THE DANGER MY ENHANCED *SPIDER-SENSE* IS WARNING ME ABOUT?

LET'S GET *SERIOUS...*

IN A DARKENED ROOM, A MAN IN AN IRON MASK NODS THOUGHTFULLY, CONSIDERING WHAT HE HAS SEEN.

'THE MAN'S NAME IS *DR. DOOM.*

HE IS PREPARING AN *ACT OF VENGEANCE.*

CHAPTER 3

CUNNING ATTRACTIONS!

JUST *LOOK* AT THIS STUFF, MARY JANE!

ALL I DO IS *THINK* OF THE CHEMICAL COMPOSITION OF MY WEB FLUID-- AND THE WEBBING TURNS INTO A GIANT *SCALE MODEL* OF ITS ATOMIC STRUCTURE!

ALMOST AS IF IT COULD *READ MY MIND!*

EVERYTHING *DOES* HAPPEN FOR A REASON! FIGURE OUT WHAT THAT REASON IS, AND YOU'LL HAVE YOUR *ANSWERS*!

WELL, MAYBE YOU'RE RIGHT...

OF COURSE I AM! NOW GIVE ME A HUG AND GO CHANGE -- WE PROMISED *FLASH THOMPSON* WE'D WATCH HIM TRAIN AT THE GYM. MEANWHILE --

--I'D BETTER GET THE *BROOM* READY. IF YOUR WEBBING IS STILL NORMAL, IT'LL BE *GOO* IN AN HOUR!

SOMETIMES YOU SUPER-GUYS LEAVE SUCH A *MESS*....!

HARD TO BELIEVE THERE WAS A TIME I *WASN'T* MARRIED TO MARY JANE, HOW DID I GET BY WITHOUT HER STRENGTH?

STILL, I SURE WISH I KNEW WHAT--

-- THE DEVIL IS GOING ON ?!

BUGLE

Wednesday, October 4, 1989

SPIDER-MAN GETS DEADLY POWERS

WEB-HEAD WASTES WILD WOMAN

PHOTO: NICK KATZENBERG

ELSEWHERE IN MANHATTAN; WHERE THREE OF THE MOST POWERFUL MEN ON THIS PLANET--

--LISTEN TO A FOURTH: *THE WIZARD!*

GRAVITON BESTED SPIDER-MAN HANDILY! BUT WHEN WE SENT TITANIA AND TRAPSTER TO FINISH THE JOB, THEY WERE *ROUTED!*

AS NEW YORK'S *KING-PIN,* I KNOW THE WEB-SLINGER BETTER THAN ANY OF US! HE'S *NEVER* BEEN THIS FORMIDABLE!

IF OUR *ACTS OF VENGEANCE* ARE TO BE SUCCESSFUL, OUR TARGETS MUST BE DESTROYED UTTERLY! BUT WHO CAN WE SEND THAT WOULD BE *POWERFUL* ENOUGH TO--

I'LL GO.

YOU, *MAGNETO?* BUT ISN'T YOUR BECOMING *DIRECTLY* INVOLVED RATHER,...

...UNUSUAL?

THESE ARE UNUSUAL CIRCUM-STANCES, *DR. DOOM.*

AND I HAVE... *PERSONAL* INTERESTS.

AS DO *I,* MUTANT! AND IF *YOURS* CONFLICT WITH *MY OWN*--

--PERHAPS THEY MAY NECESSITATE *MY* DIRECT INVOLVEMENT!

SHORTLY...
MY ALLIANCE WITH THE OTHERS IS A MATTER OF CONVENIENCE, A SUBTLE PREPARATION--

--FOR THE INEVITABLE WAR THAT DRAWS CLOSER EVERY DAY!

THE FINAL BATTLE BETWEEN HUMANKIND AND MUTANTKIND, FROM WHICH ONLY ONE SHALL EMERGE VICTORIOUS!

AND SPIDER-MAN MAY BE AN UNWITTING KEY TO THAT OUTCOME--

--IF, AS I SUSPECT, HIS NEW POWERS ARE THE RESULT OF MUTANT TRAITS MANIFESTING THEMSELVES LATE IN LIFE!

EVEN AS DID MY OWN!

IF SPIDER-MAN WERE TO JOIN OUR CAUSE, HIS POWER COULD TIP THE BALANCE, AND ASSURE TRIUMPH FOR--

HEY, MAN, HALLOWEEN AIN'T FOR TWO WEEKS YET!

HA-HA-HA!

AAGGHHH!

A TYPICAL URBAN BORE.

ONE EASILY DISPOSED OF--

--BY THE MASTER OF MAGNETIC FORCE!

H-HEADPHONES SQUEEZED TOGETHER! L-LIKE A VISE!

LOUSY MAIL-ORDER PIECE OF JUNK! I'M GONNA SUE!

53

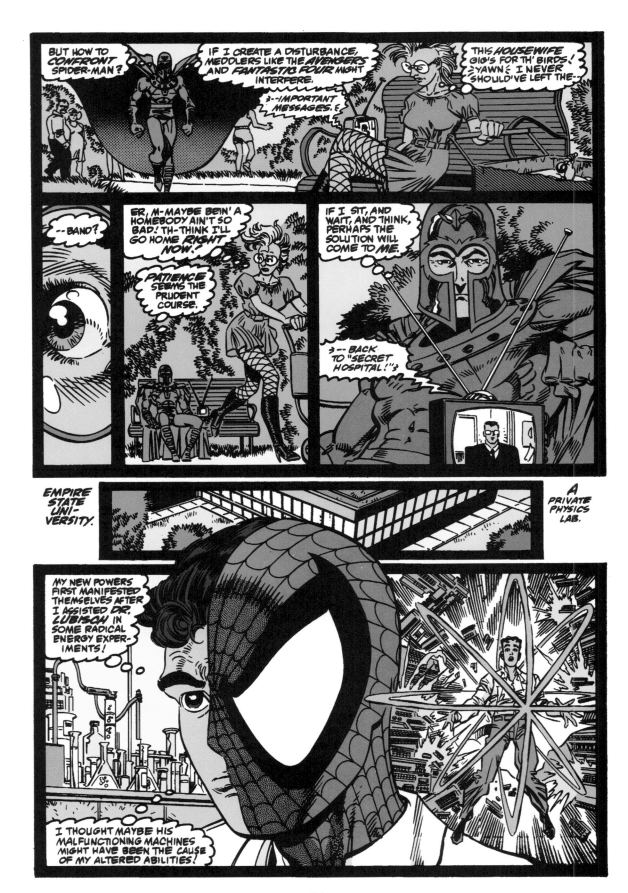

BUT I'VE CHECKED THE EQUIPMENT OUT, AND WHILE IT'S CAPABLE OF *MANIPULATING* ENERGY FIELDS, I CAN'T SEE HOW IT COULD PROJECT OR INSTILL THAT ENERGY INTO A *HUMAN BEING!*

WHICH LEAVES ME NO BETTER OFF THAN-- SOMEONE COMING!

SNOOPING, MR. PARKER?

DR. LUBISCH! UH, NO, SIR! I-I JUST WONDERED IF YOU NEEDED ANY *HELP!*

MATA HARI USED THE SAME LINE! YOUR ASSISTANCE IS NO LONGER REQUIRED, MR. PARKER.

GOOD DAY!

WELP, NOTHING THERE, BUT MAYBE I CAN LEARN SOMETHING BY *TESTING* MY NEW POWERS!

AND, TO THAT END--

--AT AN AUTOMOBILE WRECKING YARD ON THE BROOKLYN WATERFRONT...

MAN, THINGS ARE GETTIN' TIGHT! GOTTA ASK THE BOSS FOR A *RAISE* BEFORE--

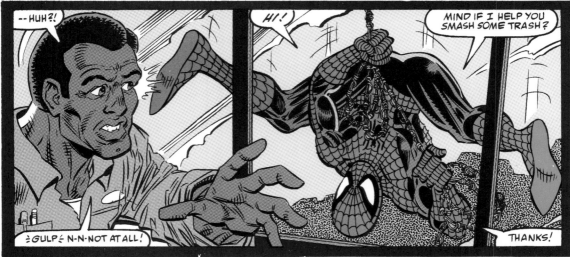

--HUH?!

HI!

MIND IF I HELP YOU SMASH SOME TRASH?

≟GULP≟ N-N-NOT AT ALL!

THANKS!

56

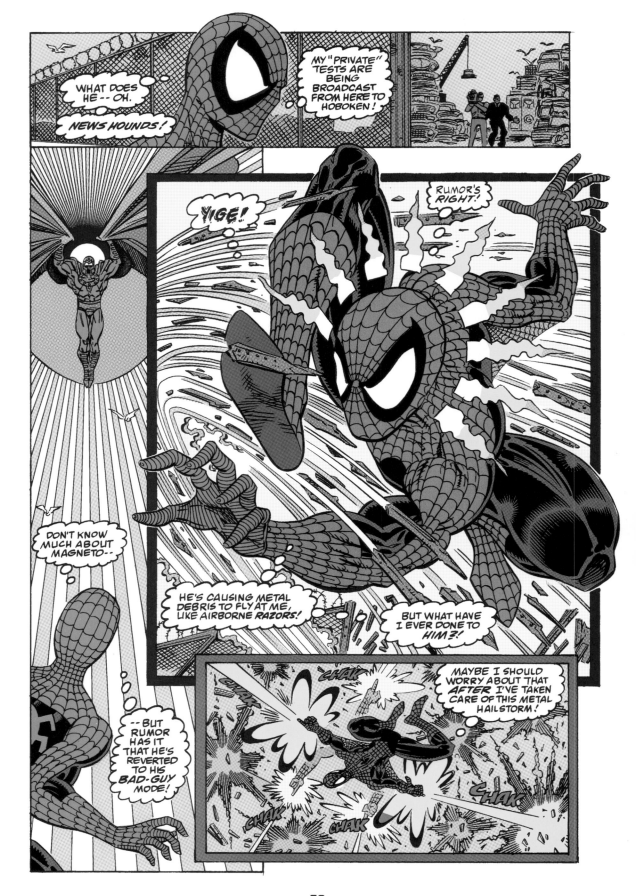

58

WAIT A MINUTE!

MY ENHANCED HEARING! PICKING UP--

--SCREAMS FOR HELP!

"IF I CAN STAY AWAY FROM MAGNETO LONG ENOUGH, MY SPIFFY NEW *TELESCOPIC VISION* SHOULD BE ABLE TO CHECK OUT--"

"--OH, LORD! I WAS WRONG! THAT CAR *DID* HURT SOMEONE OUT IN THE MIDDLE OF THE BAY!"

"IT HIT A *CRUISE SHIP!*"

BOAT'S SINKING! PEOPLE WILL *DIE!*

BECAUSE OF THE WAY I USED MY *POWERS!*

AND THERE'S NOT A BLASTED THING I CAN DO! WEB-LINES WON'T *REACH* THAT FAR! IF ONLY I COULD--

--FLY?!

AW, GEEZ!

WON'T THIS *EVER* END?

IT IS TIME FOR THIS TO END.

COME ON, HON, BUCK UP. FROM WHAT YOU TOLD ME, YOU ULTIMATELY USED YOUR NEW POWERS TO *SAVE LIVES!*

IT'S HOW IT'S *USED* -- AND *WHO* USES IT.

I KNOW, I GUESS. BUT I'M HUMAN, MJ. I MAKE MISTAKES.

SURE, I SAVED LIVES *THIS* TIME. BUT WHAT ABOUT...

SPARE COSTUME.

DON'T EVEN FEEL LIKE PUTTING IT ON.

AND IT'S NOT THE POWER ITSELF THAT'S IMPORTANT, ANYWAY.

...NEXT TIME?

CHAPTER 4

THIS IS THE CITY, LOS ANGELES, CALIFORNIA.

THIS IS THE JAIL, LOS ANGELES COUNTY JAIL.

LOS ANG COUNTY JAI

THESE ARE THE MEN, REAL ESTATE AGENTS PERCY AND BARTON GRIMES.

THOUGH THERE ARE SOME WHO SAY REAL ESTATE PRICES IN LOS ANGELES ARE A CRIME --

-- PERCY AND BARTON GRIMES ARE NOT IN PRISON FOR OVER-PRICING HOUSES IN A SELLER'S MARKET.

NOT QUITE.

RRUMBLE

AW, NO -- NOT ANOTHER EARTHQUAKE.

I JUST FINISHED RE-SURFACING MY PATIO AFTER THE LAST ONE --!

UH, BERNIE -- I COULD BE WRONG --

" -- BUT I DON'T THINK THIS IS A QUAKE.

RRRUMBLE

"ACTUALLY, BERN, IT FEELS LIKE SOMETHING'S RIPPING THE ROOF OFF -- "

SHEESH! I DIDN'T MEAN LITERALLY!

KROOM

NO, PERCY AND BARTON GRIMES ARE NOT IN LOCK-UP FOR THEIR DEEDS IN THE DEED BUSINESS.

VILE THOUGH THEIR ECONOMIC CRIMES MAY BE, PERCY AND BARTON GRIMES ARE FELONS FOR QUITE *ANOTHER REASON...*

...AND IT IS *THIS REASON* WHICH HAS BROUGHT *THIS MAN* TO L.A.

GREETINGS!

WHAT'S GOING ON? HOW'D WE GET UP HERE?

YEAH! AND WHO THE HECK ARE *YOU?* WHAT DO YOU *WANT?*

SO *MANY* QUESTIONS, SO *LITTLE* TIME.

TO ANSWER IN ORDER: THIS IS A *JAILBREAK--*

-- I RAISED YOUR CELL USING A SET OF *ANTI-GRAVITY DISKS!*

-- YOU MAY CALL ME *THE WIZARD--*

-- AND I WISH TO OFFER AN *EXCHANGE.*

OUR COSTUMES! WHERE'D YOU GET 'EM?

FROM THE *PROPERTY WAREHOUSE!*

NOW, LISTEN. A GROUP OF LIKE-MINDED MEN HAVE JOINED TO COMMIT *ACTS OF VENGEANCE* AGAINST EACH OTHER'S ENEMIES.

WE DESTROY YOUR ENEMY, IRON MAN--

AND IN RETURN, THE *BROTHERS GRIMM* DESTROY ONE OF YOURS, EH?

FAIR DEAL. WHO DO WE *KILL?*

WE WERE THINKING... SPIDER-MAN.

TWENTY-FOUR HOURS LATER, 3,000 MILES AWAY...

WELL, *ONE* GOOD POINT ABOUT THE LAST COUPLE OF DAYS, SINCE THAT ACCIDENT IN THE *EMPIRE UNIVERSITY PHYSICS LAB* ZAPPED ME WITH A LOAD OF NEW *POWER*...

MY LIFE CERTAINLY HAS GOTTEN INTERESTING.

"THESE SHATTERED SENSES"

OR "A TALE OF THE ~ Brothers Grimm"

70

I BEAT *THE TRAPSTER, TITANIA* AND *MAGNETO,* USING AN INNER ENERGY I DON'T UNDERSTAND-- --MY *SPIDER-SENSES* HAVE INCREASED ALMOST TO THE *PAIN THRESHHOLD*--

--AND, AS USUAL, I'M SO WORRIED ABOUT DOING WHAT'S *RIGHT,* I CAN'T--

SKQUAWK

HI, BIRD.

BIRD?

WHERE AM I?

OHMIGOSH...

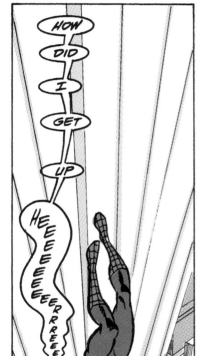

HOW DID I GET UP HEEEEEEERRREEE

THWIPP

FFRTTT

SWOOOSH

PTHUNK

OWW!

THIS IS *REALLY* GETTING OUT OF HAND.

EVERY TIME I BLINK, I'M USING SOME *EXTRA* POWER I DIDN'T KNOW I HAD.

NOW IT'S FLYING-- BUT WHAT'S NEXT?

HOW POWERFUL AM I, AND WHEN WILL I--

≥YAAAH!≤

SPIDER-SENSE ROARING-- SO PAINFUL--

--WARNING ME--

A SPY CAMERA?

HMM.

THIS IS THE SECOND TIME I FELT MYSELF BEING WATCHED IN THE LAST COUPLE OF DAYS.

SOMEBODY ELSE MUST BE AS *CURIOUS* ABOUT THE NEW MODEL WEB-SLINGER AS I AM.

WHO--?

TERRIFIC.

MY WEBLINE BARELY *GRAZED* IT--

--AND THE GADGET *BLEW UP!*

WHOEVER MADE THAT DEVICE DIDN'T WANT IT *EXAMINED.*

" SO I GUESS, FOR NOW, MY WATCHER'S *IDENTITY* WILL JUST HAVE TO REMAIN ONE OF LIFE'S LITTLE *MYSTERIES...*"

UNFORTUNATE.

KLIK

I HOPED TO PROBE SPIDER-MAN'S UNUSUAL NEW ABILITIES FROM AFAR--

--TO LEARN THEIR EXTENT AND THEIR GENESIS.

SOMEHOW, I MUST SUBVERT THAT RESOURCE TO THE SERVICE OF DR. DOOM.

MY ALLIES IN THESE ACTS OF VENGEANCE SEE THE WEB-SPINNER ONLY AS AN ENEMY TO BE ANNIHILATED.

WHAT I SEE IS A RESOURCE OF UNKNOWN AND INEXPLICABLE POTENTIAL.

≥BEEP≤ THE WIZARD REPORTING ON CHANNEL 3.

SPEAK.

GREETINGS, DOCTOR.

AS ARRANGED, I MADE CONTACT WITH THE BROTHERS GRIMM IN LOS ANGELES.

THEY'VE AGREED TO JOIN OUR ALLIANCE.

THE WEB-SLINGER WON'T KNOW WHAT HIT HIM.

WITH OUR MAGIC-BASED TALENTS, WE'LL TAKE HIM COMPLETELY BY SURPRISE.

OF COURSE YOU WILL.

MAY I SUGGEST A STRATEGY?

"COMPUTER ANALYSIS OF SPIDER-MAN'S EXPLOITS IN MANHATTAN INDICATE A CONCENTRATION OF ACTIVITY IN THE LOWER MIDTOWN AREA.

"TAKE ACTION THERE, AND IF YOU DON'T FIND HIM..."

... THE ODDS ARE EXCELLENT HE'LL FIND YOU.

AND WHEN HE DOES...

... DOOM WILL BE WATCHING.

MIDTOWN MANHATTAN, A SHORT TIME LATER...

UNGH! ANOTHER ATTACK! THE PAIN IS GETTING WORSE! HEAD FEELS LIKE IT'S GOING TO EXPLODE!

MY SPIDER-SENSE IS SHRIEKING SO LOUD--

-- I FEEL AS IF IT'S PIERCING MY SKULL WITH A LASER!

BEFORE PROFESSOR LUBISCH'S HAYWIRE EXPERIMENT, MY SPIDER-SENSE ONLY WARNED ME OF PERSONAL DANGER.

NOW, IT SETS OFF ALARMS AT THE SLIGHTEST PROVOCATION, AND I CAN'T KEEP FROM RESPONDING: MICE CRAWLING IN MY BEDROOM WALL--PIGEONS FLUTTERING PAST A BATHROOM WINDOW.

LAST NIGHT I SCARED MARY JANE HALF TO DEATH WHEN I WENT CRASHING OUT OF BED TO AVOID A MOTH.

I'VE GOT TO GET CONTROL OF MYSELF.

WHEN THESE SHATTERED SENSES START AFFECTING MY MARRIAGE, THAT'S WHERE I--

HUH? IS THAT WHAT TINGLED MY SPIDER-SENSE?

SOMETHING HAPPENING TO MADISON SQUARE GARDEN--?

RRRUMBLE

74

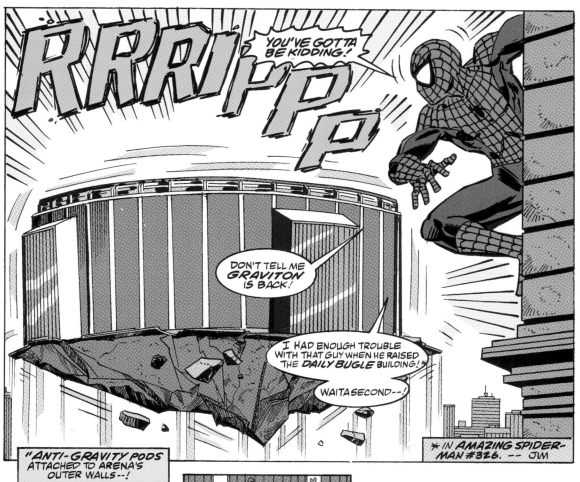

RRRIPP

YOU'VE GOTTA BE KIDDING!

DON'T TELL ME *GRAVITON* IS BACK!

I HAD ENOUGH TROUBLE WITH THAT GUY WHEN HE RAISED THE *DAILY BUGLE* BUILDING!*

WAIT A SECOND--!

*IN *AMAZING SPIDER-MAN* #326. -- JIM

"ANTI-GRAVITY PODS ATTACHED TO ARENA'S OUTER WALLS--!"

"I'VE SEEN PODS LIKE THAT BEFORE! THEY BELONG TO *THE WIZARD,* TRAPSTER'S OLD BOSS!*"

* SPIDEY BATTLED THE WIZARD IN *AMAZING SPIDER-MAN* #213. --JIM

SO THIS ISN'T *GRAVITON* WORK, AFTER ALL...

BIG DIFFERENCE *THAT* MAKES TO THOSE PEOPLE.

TIME ENOUGH TO WORRY ABOUT THE *WIZARD'S REASON* FOR RAISING MADISON SQUARE GARDEN *AFTER* I SAVE SOME LIVES.

HERE'S WHERE MY NEW POWERS *REALLY* COME IN HANDY...

75

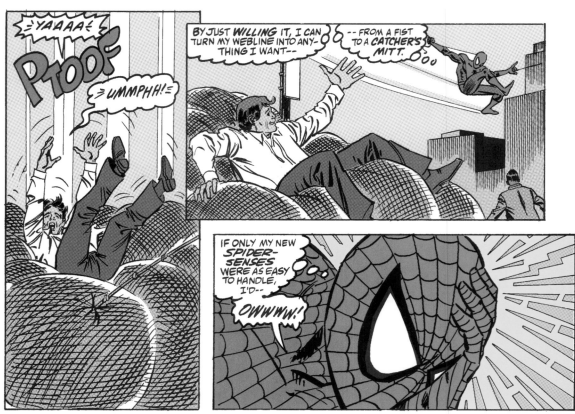

SPTOOSH

≷YUGH≷

SPIDER-MAN! OMIGOSH, WHAT'S THAT STUFF AROUND YOUR HEAD?

FEELS LIKE COTTON CANDY--

≷COUGH ≷CHOKE≷

--WORKS LIKE TEAR GAS!

≷COUGH≷ YOU FOLKS BETTER FIND SOME SHELTER-- ≷CHOKE≷

CALL IT A HUNCH-- ≷GASP≷

"--BUT I BET THINGS ARE GOING TO GET PRETTY NASTY AROUND HERE IN THE NEXT FEW MINUTES..."

I SAY IT'LL FLOAT.

AND I SAY IT WON'T.

BROTHER, YOU'RE SUCH A PESSIMIST.

HOW MAY WE ADJUDICATE THIS DIFFERENCE OF OPINION?

THE WIZARD SAID, IF WE WANTED TO ERADICATE HIS ANTI-GRAV PODS.

--WE ONLY HAD TO PRESS THIS LITTLE BUTTON.

ALLOW ME.

BY ALL MEANS.

KLK

THE LAST COUPLE OF DAYS, I'VE BEEN A *PUNCHING BAG* FOR EVERY COSTUMED FELON IN THE TRI-STATE AREA WITH TIME ON HIS HANDS AND A BUG UP HIS NOSE.

GRAVITON, TRAPSTER, TITANIA, MAGNETO-- THESE TWO GOONS CALLED *GRIMM*--

THEY ALL WANTED A *PIECE* OF ME, AND I DON'T KNOW *WHY.*

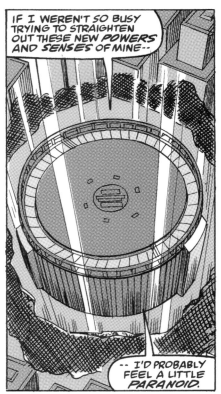

IF I WEREN'T SO BUSY TRYING TO STRAIGHTEN OUT THESE NEW *POWERS* AND *SENSES* OF MINE--

--I'D PROBABLY FEEL A LITTLE *PARANOID.*

INSTEAD, WHAT I FEEL IS--

--*TICKED OFF!*

I *TOLD* YOU THE ARENA WOULDN'T FLOAT.

BUT YOU *DIDN'T* TELL ME THE WEB-SLINGER WOULD *CATCH* IT!

NEITHER DID *THE WIZARD!*

SPIDER-MAN IS MUCH *STRONGER* THAN WE WERE LED TO BELIEVE.

NOTICED THAT, DID YOU?

SUDDENLY, BROTHER--

"-- OUR LITTLE *TRADE-OFF* DOESN'T SEEM LIKE SUCH A *BARGAIN* AFTER ALL."

OWW!
OWW!
OWW!
OWW!

EVERY MOVE I MAKE, EVERY BREATH I TAKE, MY SPIDER-SENSE *STINGS* ME WITH A WARNING:

TOO MANY WARNINGS, MASKING *REAL* DANGER LIKE *STATIC* ON A PHONE LINE!

WELL? HE'S *GAINING* ON US. *THINK* OF SOMETHING!

YOU THINK OF SOMETHING-- MOTHER ALWAYS SAID *YOU* WERE THE *SMART* ONE.

HEAD HURTS SO BAD-- BUT I'VE GOT TO *CONCENTRATE,* GOT TO IGNORE THE *FALSE FEELINGS!*

NEVER THOUGHT HAVING *TOO MUCH POWER* COULD BE SUCH A *PAIN...*

-- AND MAN DOES IT FEEL GOOD!

CRASH

"FROM NOW ON, NO MATTER WHAT MY SPIDER-SENSE TELLS ME, I'M GOING TO CHOOSE MY OWN REACTIONS,"

NO MORE REACTING BY INSTINCT, NO MORE SUBCONSCIOUS SURPRISE FLIGHTS, NO MORE--

83

FFFWIPP

PTOOM

I-I DIDN'T MEAN TO DO THAT. I WANTED THAT SPY CAMERA IN ONE PIECE.

BUT MY BODY JUST-- *REACTED.*

WHAT'S *HAPPENED* TO ME?

HMMM.

IF THE TELEMETRY READINGS TRANSMITTED BY MY MONITOR BEFORE ITS DESTRUCTION ARE *CORRECT--*

-- SPIDER-MAN IS IMBUED WITH AN ENERGY FIELD SO GREAT, IT IS BEYOND THE CAPACITY OF MY INSTRUMENTS TO *CALIBRATE.*

I WANT THAT *POWER.*

BY RIGHT, IT IS *MINE.*

FOR ULTIMATE POWER IS THE ULTIMATE DESTINY OF *DOOM.*

EPILOGUE:

A LOFT APARTMENT IN MANHATTAN'S *SOHO* DISTRICT...

⸚BEEP!⸚ HI, HUBBY HON -- IT'S M.J.

GOTTA WORK TONIGHT --

-- SO FORAGE DINNER WITHOUT ME, OKAY?

AND DON'T WAIT UP. THE GIRLS AND I ARE MEETING FOR COFFEE AND TALK TILL LATE.

LOVE 'YA!

⸚BEEEP!⸚

ALL THE POWER I'VE GOT, AND AT THE END OF THE DAY, HERE I AM ALONE,...

... EATING A LUKEWARM TV DINNER IN FRONT OF THE TUBE...

... WASHING IT DOWN WITH A SOUR DOSE OF SELF-PITY.

THE TRUTH IS, I'M *SCARED.*

I HAVE POWERS I CAN'T *PREDICT* OR *COMMAND.*

MY LIFE IS OUT OF CONTROL AND IT FRIGHTENS ME.

BUT, HEY --! THINGS COULD BE WORSE.

I *COULD* BE NICK KATZENBERG,...

CHAPTER 5

ON THE VERY BEST OF DAYS, EVENING RUSH HOUR ON NEW YORK'S TRIBORO BRIDGE IS A DELIRIUM OF TRAFFIC SNARLS, SHORT TEMPERS, FENDER BENDERS AND MUTTERED CURSES.

ADD AN INDIAN SUMMER HEAT WAVE, CONSTRUCTION WORK ON THE MAJOR DEEGAN EXPRESSWAY INTO NEW ENGLAND...

...NOT TO MENTION A PAIR OF SUPER-POWERED NON-MUTANTS DUKING IT OUT OVER THE TOLL BOOTH PLAZA...

...AND THERE YOU HAVE A RECIPE FOR A FIRST-CLASS NEW YORK DISASTER.

THE HARDER THEY FALL

THAT'S LIFE IN THE BIG CITY.

SO TO SPEAK,

TOLL MACHINE

EXACT NO BILLS NO PENNIES

MANNED LANE

OKAY, YOU'VE MADE YOUR *POINT*, BIG FELLA.

YOU'RE EVERY BIT AS TOUGH AS *THE TRAPSTER, TITANIA, GRAVITRON* AND *THE BROTHERS GRIMM* --

-- BUT I'VE GOT JUST AS MUCH REASON TO FIGHT *YOU* AS I HAD TO FIGHT THEM :

NAMELY, *NONE!*

SO WHY DON'T WE CALL IT QUITS BEFORE ONE OF US GETS *HURT?*

BTOOM

KEEP *TALKIN'*, SQUIRT! THE MADDER YOU MAKE ME, THE HARDER I HIT!

'SCUSE ME FOR BEIN' A NIT-PICK, *GOLIATH* --

-- BUT ISN'T THAT THE *HULK'S* OLD LINE?

FIRST TIME I EVER BEEN GLAD TA GET CAUGHT IN A *TRAFFIC JAM.*

THESE PICS ARE GONNA SAVE MY JOB AT THE *DAILY BUGLE.*

MAN-OH-MAN! I CAN SEE THE HEADLINES *NOW...*

"SPIDER-MAN WRECKS BRIDGE IN BATTLE WITH 60-FOOT BEHEMOTH!"

"NICKIE-BOY, YOU'RE IN CLOVER! YESIREE-ROBERT!"

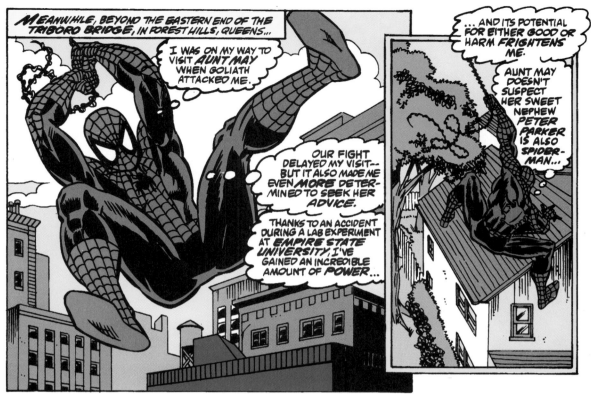

MEANWHILE, BEYOND THE EASTERN END OF THE TRIBORO BRIDGE, IN FOREST HILLS, QUEENS...

I WAS ON MY WAY TO VISIT *AUNT MAY* WHEN GOLIATH ATTACKED ME.

OUR FIGHT DELAYED MY VISIT-- BUT IT ALSO MADE ME EVEN *MORE* DETERMINED TO SEEK HER *ADVICE.*

THANKS TO AN ACCIDENT DURING A LAB EXPERIMENT AT *EMPIRE STATE UNIVERSITY,* I'VE GAINED AN INCREDIBLE AMOUNT OF *POWER...*

... AND ITS POTENTIAL FOR EITHER GOOD OR HARM *FRIGHTENS* ME.

AUNT MAY DOESN'T SUSPECT HER SWEET NEPHEW *PETER PARKER* IS ALSO *SPIDER-MAN...*

...BUT SHE'S THE WISEST PERSON I KNOW...

... AND DIRECTLY OR INDIRECTLY, I NEED HER *GUIDANCE.*

EVEN SO, I HATE TO *BOTHER* HER.

WITH *NATHAN* SUFFERING FROM A TERMINAL HEART DISEASE, THEY HAVE SO LITTLE TIME TOGETHER...

WHY, MY GOODNESS-- LOOK, NATHAN! IT'S *PETER!*

AND I JUST BAKED A BATCH OF HIS FAVORITE COOKIES...

HI, AUNT MAY-- HI, NATHAN.

FEELING ANY *BETTER?*

ODD THING, MY BOY. I'M DYING, BUT I HAVEN'T *FELT* THIS FINE IN YEARS.

YOU, ON THE OTHER HAND...

YEAH, I MUST LOOK PRETTY *FRAZZLED.*

ACTUALLY, THAT'S WHY I'M HERE, AUNT MAY.

NATHAN?

YOU TWO TAKE A WALK.

I'LL FINISH WITH THESE *LEAVES.*

I NEED TO TALK.

HOW'S NATHAN FEELING *REALLY,* AUNT MAY?

WEAKER THAN HE LETS ON, PETER--

-- BUT WE'VE BOTH COME TO *ACCEPT* THE INEVITABLE.

NOW. WHAT'S TROUBLING *YOU?*

YOU HAVEN'T BROUGHT ME A *PROBLEM* SINCE YOU WERE A LITTLE BOY.

I HAVEN'T, HAVE I?

NO, YOU ALWAYS TRIED TO BE *STRONG* FOR ME, PETER.

PERHAPS *TOO* STRONG.

HOW CAN I HELP?

WELL... JUST AS A *HYPOTHETICAL QUESTION,* AUNT MAY...

... WHAT WOULD YOU DO IF YOU HAD THE POWER OF *LIFE AND DEATH?*

SOMEWHERE ELSE.

IN A PLACE OF ICE COLD DARKNESS...

...SHATTERED BY A SINGLE CONE OF WHITE HOT LIGHT.

GOLIATH.

SUCH A GRANDIOSE NAME FOR SUCH AN ABYSMAL FAILURE.

GIVE ME ANOTHER CRACK-- ANOTHER CHANCE--

ANOTHER CHANCE TO FLOUNDER?

THESE ARE ACTS OF VENGEANCE, NOT MERCY.

HE'S STRONGER THAN YOU SAID HE'D BE, MAGNETO!

I'D BEAT HIM IF I HAD THE POWER.

PERHAPS THERE IS A WAY.

IN THESE ACTS OF VENGEANCE, BY TRADING FOES WE DO NOT USUALLY OPPOSE, WE SEEK TO GAIN TACTICAL AND STRATEGIC ADVANTAGE OVER OUR ENEMIES.

A PROJECT OF THIS KIND DEMANDS CAREFUL PLANNING AND KNOWN QUANTITIES.

SPIDER-MAN IS NO LONGER A KNOWN QUANTITY.

YOU SAID... MAYBE THERE'S A WAY--?

FOR DOCTOR DOOM THERE IS ALWAYS A WAY TO SEIZE VICTORY FROM DEFEAT.

AND AT THE SAME TIME, PERHAPS GAIN A PERMANENT ADVANTAGE OVER MY TEMPORARY ALLIES...

FOREST HILLS.

A PLACE OF *WARM LIGHT* AMID GATHERING SHADOWS...

I DIDN'T WANT TO *SHOCK* YOU, AUNT MAY.

I ONLY MEANT IT AS A HYPOTHETICAL QUESTION--

THE POWER OF *LIFE AND DEATH*, PETER-- THAT'S A *GOD-LIKE* POWER.

NO HUMAN BEING SHOULD *CARRY* SUCH A BURDEN, EVEN "HYPOTHETICALLY."

BURDEN?

THE ABILITY TO SAVE LIVES IS A *BURDEN...?*

WHICH LIVES? HOW DO YOU CHOOSE?

THE *SEASONS* OF LIFE ARE A CYCLE, PETER-- SPRING BIRTH, SUMMER GROWTH, AUTUMNAL AGE, AND WINTERY DEATH.

WHEN YOU NEAR THE END OF THE CYCLE YOU SEE THE WISDOM, THE *BEAUTY* OF IT ALL.

I *ACCEPT* AGE AND DEATH, PETER.

I ACCEPTED YOUR UNCLE BEN'S DEATH, SHOCK THOUGH IT WAS, AND WHEN NATHAN'S TIME COMES--

-- OR *MY* TIME -- I'LL ACCEPT THAT TOO.

ACCEPTANCE, DEAR BOY, IS THE ONLY POWER OF LIFE AND DEATH A HUMAN BEING EVER NEEDS.

THANKS, AUNT MAY.

RAIN CHECK ON THOSE COOKIES?

ANY TIME, MY DEAR, DEAR BOY.

94

AN HOUR LATER. MANHATTAN. THE DAILY BUGLE BUILDING.

SO WHADDAYA SAY, TOM? DID NICKIE DELIVER THE *GOODS* OR WHAT?

I WOULD PREFER YOU ADDRESS ME AS *MR. FIREHEART*, MR. KATZENBERG.

MS. CUSHING, AS THE DAILY BUGLE'S NEW *MANAGING EDITOR*, HOW WOULD *YOU* DESCRIBE THESE PHOTOS?

THEY SHOW SPIDER-MAN WRECKING THE *TRIBORO BRIDGE* DURING A BATTLE--

-- WITH APPARENT DISREGARD FOR THE *SAFETY* OF NEARBY COMMUTERS.

JOURNALISTICALLY SPEAKING, THEY'RE *DYNAMITE.*

EXACTLY.

SO DO YOU *LOVE* 'EM? DO I GET A *RAISE*? HOW MUCH?

A RAISE?

MR. KATZENBERG, COUNT YOURSELF LUCKY I LET YOU DRAW A *SALARY!*

SPIDER-MAN IS A *HERO.* BRING ME PHOTOS LIKE PETER PARKER'S-- THAT *REFLECT* SPIDER-MAN'S HEROISM--

--OR FIND A *NEW* JOB.

KATE, WE NEVER BEEN FRIENDS-- BUT YOU GOTTA *DO* SOMETHING!

FIREHEART'S WORSE THAN JAMESON *EVER* WAS!

SORRY, NICK. I CAN'T HELP YOU.

SELL-OUT. SINCE FIREHEART PROMOTED HER, KATE'S BEEN A REAL *MOUSE.*

FACE IT, NICK--

"-- THANKS TO THOMAS FIREHEART, THIS OLD GRAY *PAPER* JUST AIN'T WHAT SHE USED TO BE!"

EH?

WHAT ARE *YOU* DOING IN MY *PRIVATE* OFFICE?

GET OUT.

HEY, IS THAT ANY WAY TO GREET *"NEW YORK'S GREATEST UNSUNG HERO"?*

I'VE BEEN READING YOUR *EDITORIALS,* TOMMY.

I DON'T KNOW WHETHER TO FEEL TOUCHED, FLATTERED, OR *NAUSEATED.*

I SAID, GET OUT.

NOT TILL YOU ANSWER ME *ONE* QUESTION.

WHEN WILL YOU QUIT PROMOTING ME AS NEW YORK'S ANSWER TO *MOTHER THERESA* AND SELL THE BUGLE BACK TO JONAH JAMESON?

WHEN I'VE REHABILITATED YOUR *REPUTATION,* AND DISCHARGED MY DEBT OF *HONOR* TO YOU.

NOW, FOR THE *FINAL* TIME-- EH?

MISS GRANT...

SIR, PHONE CALL ON LINE ONE-- IT SOUNDS *URGENT!*

...

THE *LAST* TIME GLORIA GRANT SAW SPIDER-MAN, SHE TRIED TO KILL HIM TO SAVE HER LOVER, THE GANGSTER EDUARDO LOBO.

HER GUNSHOT WENT *WILD...*

...AND HER LOVER WAS THE ONE TO DIE.

IT IS A *SECRET* SHE AND THE WEB-SPINNER SHARE.

SEEING HIM REMINDS HER BOTH OF THE SECRET...

...AND OF A *GRIEF* SHE CANNOT BEAR.

I'VE SAID ALL I *INTEND* TO SAY TO YOU, WEB-SPINNER. IF YOU DON'T MIND, I HAVE A PHONE CALL TO TAKE.

MAYBE *YOU'RE* FINISHED WITH THIS CONVERSATION, BUT I'M--

KINGPIN?

THIS IS *WEIRD?*

ALL MY SENSES ARE SO *ACUTE,* I CAN HEAR THINGS THAT WOULD'VE BEEN *INAUDIBLE* ONLY A FEW DAYS AGO!

MR. *FIREHEART,* I WISH TO CONTACT SPIDER-MAN.

AS HIS FOREMOST *BOOSTER* THESE DAYS, YOU MUST HAVE THE CONNECTIONS TO--

GIMME THAT PHONE.

KINGPIN, THIS IS *SPIDER-MAN.*

ARE YOU THE GUY BEHIND THE CREEPS WHO'VE BEEN ATTACKING ME? YES OR NO?

WHAT THE--?

AH, I HOPED TO REACH YOU THROUGH AN *INTERMEDIARY,* BUT THIS IS BETTER. *MUCH* BETTER.

TONIGHT. *BATTERY PARK.* WE'LL DISCUSS OUR... SITUATION.

YOU'RE MEETING THE *KINGPIN?* TO DISCHARGE MY DEBT, I'LL JOIN YOU AS *PUMA.*

NO.

MY ENEMY. MY FIGHT.

I DON'T LIKE YOU, WEB-SLINGER. BEING IN YOUR DEBT MAKES ME... *UNCOMFORTABLE.*

BUT I THINK, AT LAST I'M BEGINNING TO *RESPECT* YOU...

BATTERY PARK.

AN HOUR PAST TWILIGHT.

KTHUMP

OKAY, SHAMU. THIS MEETING WAS *YOUR* IDEA.

WHY DID YOU ASK ME HERE?

THANKS TO YOU AND *THE LOBO BROTHERS*, SPIDER-MAN, MY AUTHORITY IN THE NEW YORK UNDERWORLD HAS BEEN *HALVED*.

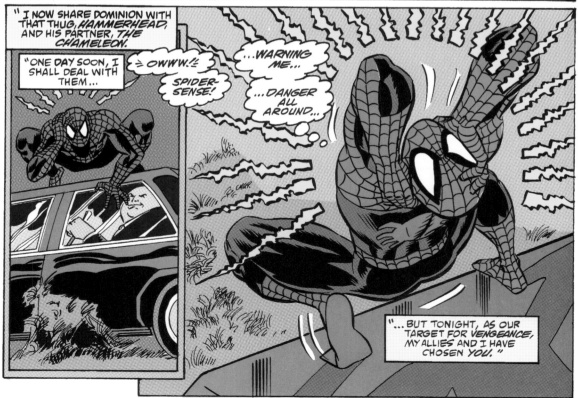

" I NOW SHARE DOMINION WITH THAT THUG, *HAMMERHEAD*, AND HIS PARTNER, *THE CHAMELEON*.

"ONE DAY SOON, I SHALL DEAL WITH THEM...

≈ OWWW.!≈

SPIDER-SENSE!

...WARNING ME...

...DANGER ALL AROUND...

"...BUT TONIGHT, AS OUR TARGET FOR *VENGEANCE*, MY ALLIES AND I HAVE CHOSEN *YOU*. "

--BIGGER THAN ANYONE'S EVER BEEN BEFORE!

THR-ROOM

YOU AND *THE KINGPIN*-- ALLIED WITH *DR. DOOM?*

WHEN DID *THAT* HAPPEN?

WHY DON'T PEOPLE *TELL* ME THESE THINGS?

THERE'S A LOT YOU DON'T KNOW, WALL-CRAWLER-- PLANS AND SECRETS YOU CAN'T EVEN *GUESS!* *KINGPIN* AND *DOOM* AND THE OTHERS-- THEY'VE GOT IT ALL FIGURED OUT--

GOLIATH, *BACK OFF!* DON'T MAKE ME *HURT* YOU!

GO AHEAD--! TAKE YOUR BEST SHOT!

YOU NEVER *LEARN*, DO YOU?

THE POWER COMES ALMOST *UNBIDDEN*...

..MORE A REFLEX THAN A CONSCIOUS ACT OF WILL.

SHA-ROOM

AND THOUGH HE TRIES TO RESTRAIN THE ENERGIES FLOWING THROUGH HIM, LIKE LIGHTNING FROM A STORM CLOUD--

--HE FINDS HE CANNOT COMMAND WHAT HE DOES NOT COMPREHEND!

AAARRGH!

FZAM

WHAT DID I DO? I JUST *IMAGINED* KNOCKING GOLIATH OFF HIS FEET-- AND THAT *ENERGY BEAM* SHOT FROM MY EYES!

MY GOD, DID I KILL HIM?!

NO! HE'S STILL STANDING!

"HUH? HE ISN'T JUST STANDING, HE'S *GROWING!* SIXTY FEET, SEVENTY-FIVE, A HUNDRED--"

"TWO HUNDRED FEET!"

"HOW DID HE DO *THAT*?"

IN A PLACE OF COLD DARKNESS, A MAN IN STEEL GRAY ARMOR NODS WITH GRATIFICATION.

MONITORS BLINK WITH IMAGES OF FAR-OFF BATTLE.

INSTRUMENTS FLICKER WITH READINGS OF INCREDIBLE POWER.

SATISFACTORY.

AS INTENDED, THE MECHANISM I IMPLANTED IN GOLIATH'S PITUITARY GLAND AFTER OUR DISCUSSION THIS AFTERNOON IS *DIVERTING* SPIDER-MAN'S STRANGE NEW ENERGY FIELD--

--CHANNELING POWER *DIRECTLY* INTO GOLIATH'S CHEMICALLY-ALTERED GROWTH SYSTEM.

SPIDER-MAN'S EFFORTS TO DEFEAT GOLIATH WILL ONLY CAUSE THE GIANT TO *INCREASE* IN SIZE--

--PROVIDING ME AN OPPORTUNITY TO EXPLORE THE EXACT *NATURE* OF THE WEB-SPINNER'S ENERGY SOURCE.

ONCE I UNDERSTAND ITS NATURE...

... I WILL REASON OUT A METHOD TO *TAP* THAT POWER FOR MYSELF.

" THEN I WILL GAIN THE *ULTIMATE* ADVANTAGE OVER ALL THOSE WHO HINDER MY DESTINY, ENEMIES AND ALLIES *ALIKE.* "

WHAT DOES IT TAKE TO BRING YOU *DOWN,* BIG MAN?

MORE THAN *YOU'VE* GOT, LITTLE MAN!

WANNA *BET?*

PZAM!

=OWW=

EVERY TIME I ZAP HIM, GOLIATH GETS *BIGGER*--

--AND IT'S *HURTING* HIM MORE THAN HE KNOWS!

I CAN HEAR HIS *HEARTBEAT*-- THUDDING LIKE A RUNAWAY *JACKHAMMER!*

CAN'T KEEP THIS UP-- I'LL KILL HIM!

CAN'T-- --BREATHE--

PATTATUM
PATTATUM
PATTATUM

HIS *HEART'S* GIVING OUT!

ALL THAT GROWING-- SO QUICK-- *TOO MUCH* FOR HIM--!

PATTATUM   PATTATUM   PATTA PATTA

CAN'T

SPLASH

TIDAL WAVE --!

HE REACTS *INSTINCTIVELY* NOW, NO LONGER QUITE SO *SURPRISED* BY THE POWER HE WIELDS.

HIS IS A POWER THAT CAN BRING A GIANT TO HIS KNEES, OR TRANS-FORM A WEBLINE INTO A WAVE-*SHATTERING* WALL.

SUCH POWER CONVEYS A SPECIAL BLESSING, AND A SPECIAL *BURDEN.*

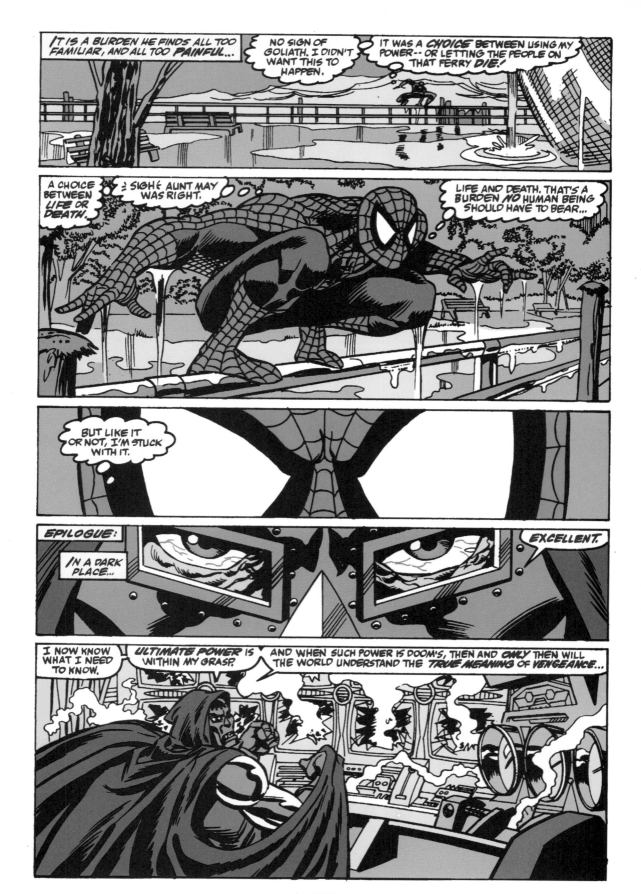

CHAPTER 6

-- OUR QUARRY IS *DANGEROUS,* AS WELL AS *VALUABLE.*

WHEN I WAS RECENTLY APPROACHED BY A GROUP OF POWERFUL MEN, TOLD THAT THEY WOULD DESTROY THE BANE OF MY EXISTENCE -- THE HELLFIRE CLUB'S *INNER CIRCLE* -- IF I WOULD ELIMINATE *SPIDER-MAN* FOR THEM...

...I WAS *INTRIGUED.*

BUT IT SOON BECAME APPARENT THAT THERE WAS MORE TO THE OFFER THAN *COMMON GAIN.*

ONE OF THEIR GROUP IS *MAGNETO,* THE MAN WHO DEPOSED ME AS *BLACK KING* OF THE *HELLFIRE CLUB!*

OUR MUTUAL HATRED APPROACHES LEGEND.

MAGNETO UNDOUBTEDLY FEELS THAT SPIDER-MAN -- WITH THE NEW, VIRTUALLY *GODLIKE* POWER HE'S REPORTED TO POSSESS -- COULD DISPOSE OF ME ONCE AND FOR ALL! AH, MY OLD ENEMY, WHEN WILL YOU LEARN...

...THAT I AM NOT *STUPID!*

WHA--?! AH, GEEZ... WHERE DO I HAVE TO GO FOR A LITTLE *PRIVACY* THESE DAYS -- THE *MOON?!*

NEW YORK: SEVERAL HOURS EARLIER, AS A RAINSTORM BLANKETS THE FIVE BOROUGHS.

AND A BLANKET OF *FEAR* COLDLY CLOAKS LIBERTY ISLAND...

TERRORISTS. THREATENING TO BLOW UP THE STATUE OF LIBERTY.

IF THIS WAS A TV SHOW, I'D SWITCH CHANNELS!

IT'S SAD, THAT SOMETHING SO *CALLOUS* HAS ALMOST BECOME *CLICHÉ.*

BUT THINGS LIKE THIS SEEM TO HAPPEN EVERY DAY. I'VE GROWN TO *ACCEPT* THEM, KNOWING THAT I CAN'T SAVE THE WHOLE *WORLD.*

EXCEPT THAT NOW, WITH MY NEW POWERS--

-- MAYBE I CAN!

I GOT NOTHING AGAINST *SPIDER-MAN*, BUT FOR THE KIND OF DOUGH SHAW'S OFFERING, I'D EVEN SKRAG *MYSELF!*

HE SAID THE *AVENGERS* AND THE OTHER TOUGH GUYS WOULD BE BUSY WITH THEIR OWN PROBLEMS, THAT THE BEST WAY TO DRAW THE WEBSLINGER OUT WOULD BE TO CAUSE A *COMMOTION!*

I'M GONNA *LIKE* THIS JOB!

SPLAP

ERNIE! D-DID I JUST SEE--

NO! AN' NEITHER DID *I!*

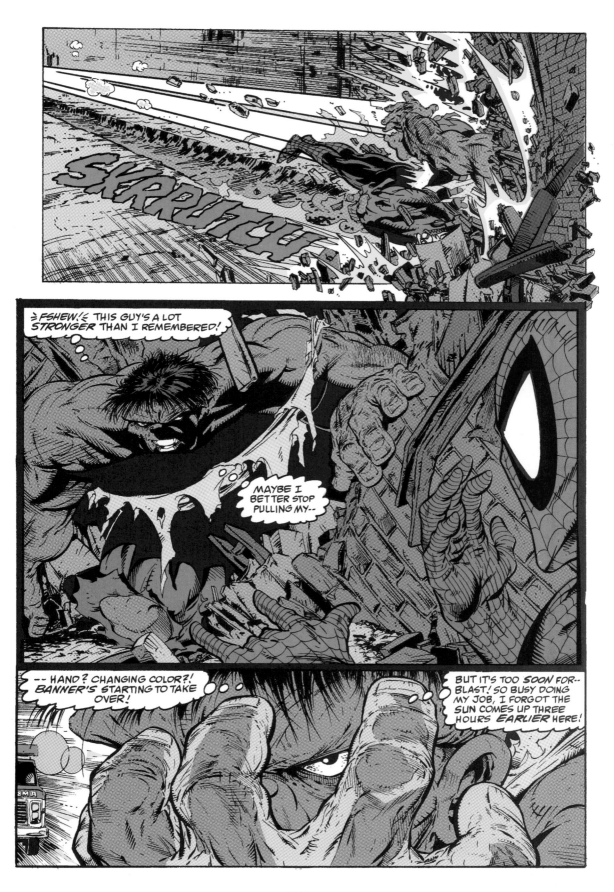

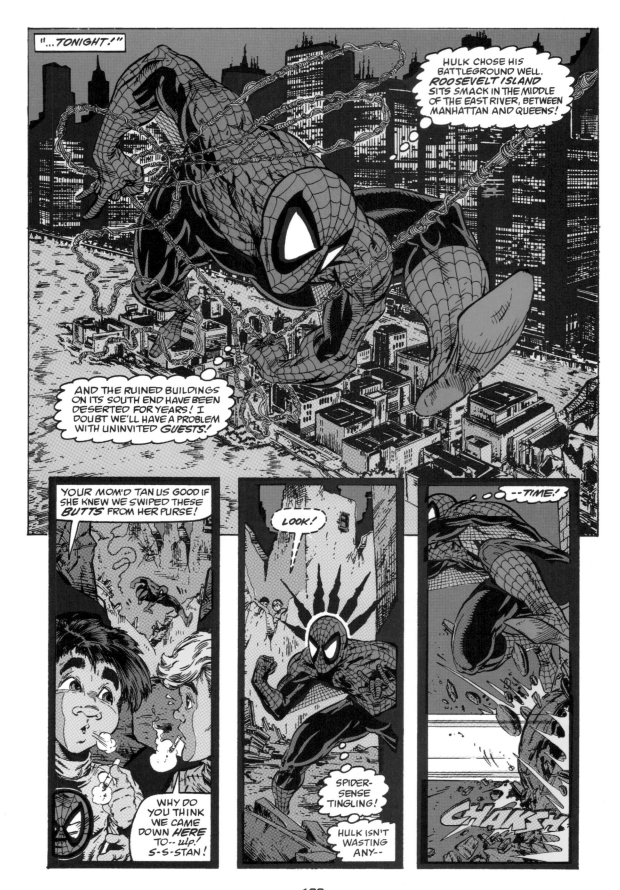

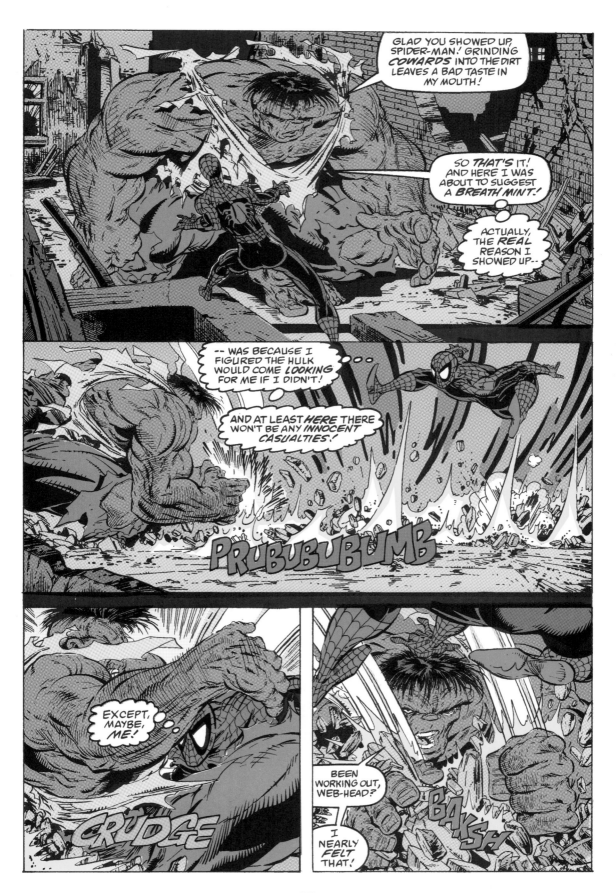

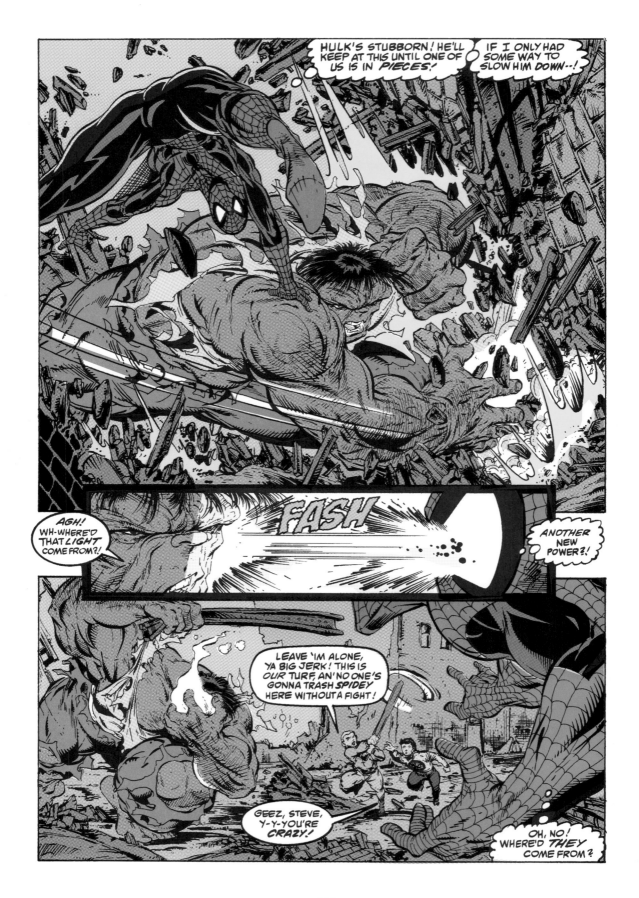

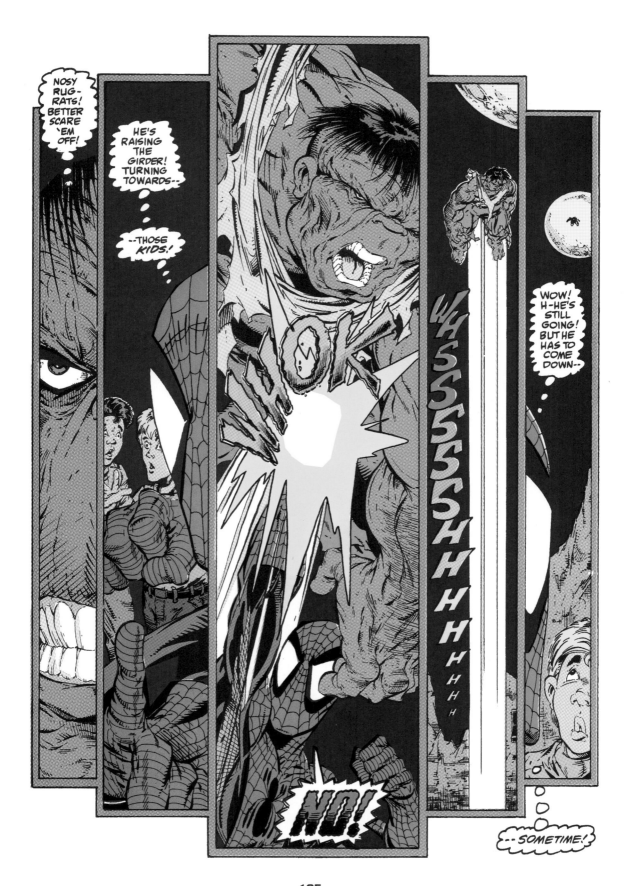

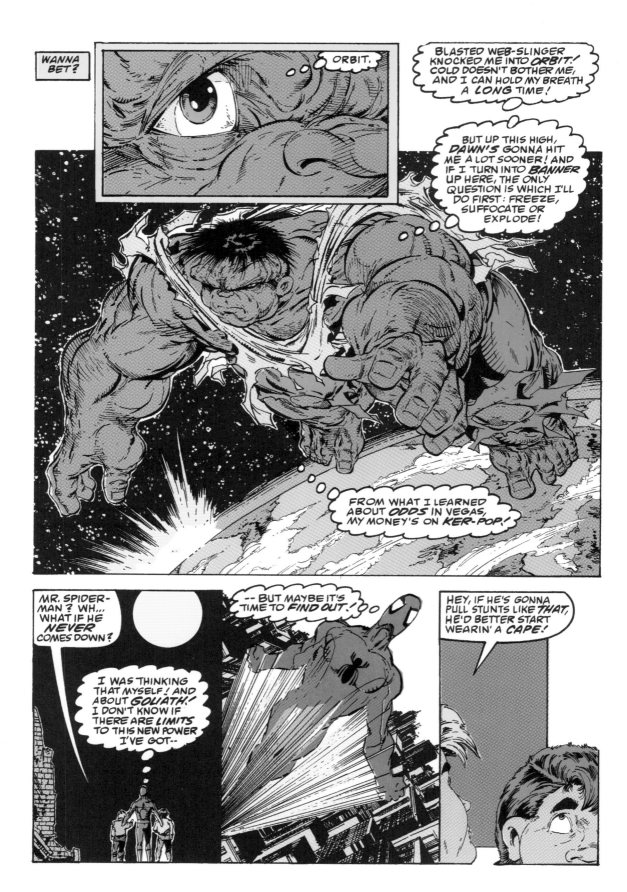

127

A THOUGHT ALMOST AS EXHILARATING AS IT IS FRIGHT-ENING, AND ONE PETER PARKER SHARES WITH HIS WIFE THE NEXT DAY.

FIRST, I MAY HAVE KILLED GOLIATH! THEN I ALMOST KILL THE HULK!

I HATE THIS NEW POWER!

I JUST WISH IT WOULD GO AWAY...

WHILE AT SHAW INDUSTRIES...

MR. BANNER IS CONFUSED.

THAT SHOULD KEEP HIM DOCILE FOR HIS TRIP BACK TO NEVADA.

BUT BANNER IS THE LEAST OF MY WORRIES. THE NEW POWERS SPIDER-MAN POSSESSES MAY BE A THREAT TO MORE THAN MAGNETO'S PETTY MACHINATIONS.

THEY MAY POSE A DANGER TO MY PLANS AS WELL! IT MIGHT BE WISE TO LOOK INTO THE PHENOMENON FURTHER, YES.

WITH DILIGENCE AND PATIENCE, PERHAPS I CAN FIND A WAY TO MAKE THOSE POWERS... GO AWAY!

CHAPTER 7

"THE FEAR AND THE FURY"
OR: "THE METAL IN MEN'S SOULS"

PROJECT POWER: (PROGRESS REPORT, CRYPTO-CODED BY VICTOR VON DOOM): "AFTER WASTING SIX HOURS SEARCHING THE OCEAN FLOOR EAST OF NEW YORK BAY...

"...MY HIRED HENCHMEN FINALLY FOUND WHAT WE WERE LOOKING FOR TWO THOUSAND FEET FROM THE NEW JERSEY SHORE.

"HOW CAN I EVER CLAIM MY DESTINY IF I HAVE TO DEPEND ON THE SERVICES OF DOLTS LIKE THESE?

"ANY *IMBECILE* WITH A TIDE AND CURRENT CHART COULD HAVE PREDICTED-- *EH?*

"THAT *FOOL!*

"HE LET THE SECONDARY RESTRAINING CLAMP *SLIP!*

"ANOTHER MOMENT, AND THE ARTIFACT WOULD HAVE *FALLEN* TO THE SEA FLOOR.

"SUCH BLATANT *INCOMPETENCE* CANNOT GO UNPUNISHED.

"FORTUNATELY FOR HIM, I'M IN A *GENEROUS* MOOD.

"I'LL LET HIM LIVE.

PTOOM

"ON SECOND THOUGHT, THERE'S NO POINT IN SETTING A POOR PRECEDENT.

"*DISCIPLINE* MUST BE ENFORCED.

"*STANDARDS* HAVE TO BE MAINTAINED,"

PROJECT POWER (PROGRESS REPORT CONTINUED):

"THE ARTIFACT APPEARS REMARKABLY *WELL-PRESERVED,* CONSIDERING THE MONTHS IT SPENT UNDERWATER...

"...NOT TO MENTION THE *DECADES* WHEN IT REMAINED 'MOTH-BALLED' BY A BUREAUCRACY TOO SHAMED TO ADMIT ITS *EXISTENCE.*

"IN OFFICIAL GOVERNMENT PAPERS, THE ARTIFACT WAS NAMED *T.E.S.S.-ONE...*

"...AN ACRONYM MEANING *TOTAL ELIMINATION OF SUPER-SOLDIERS.*

"APPARENTLY, IN THE EARLY DAYS OF *WORLD WAR TWO,* SOME SCIENTISTS FEARED THAT THE PROJECT WHICH CREATED *CAPTAIN AMERICA* MIGHT PRODUCE RENEGADE SUPER-SOLDIERS...

"THE T.E.S.S. ROBOT WAS BUILT IN ANTICIPATION OF SUCH AN IMAGINED *THREAT* TO NATIONAL SECURITY."

DR. DOOM!

KINGPIN AND MAGNETO HAVE ISSUED YOU A SUMMONS!

THEY WANT TO DISCUSS THE RISING *ANTI-SUPER-HUMAN* SENTIMENT IN CONGRESS...

TELL THEM I'LL COME WHEN I CAN, AND GO AWAY.

MORE IMPORTANT MATTERS THAN PETTY *POLITICS* CONCERN ME NOW.

"INDEED.

"TODAY I TAKE STEPS TO SEAL MY *DESTINY.*"

TIMES SQUARE.

MID-AFTERNOON.

THERE USED TO BE CERTAIN *RULES* IN THE SUPER-VILLAIN COMMUNITY, MOSTLY UNSPOKEN, BUT GENERALLY ACCEPTED.

"STAY OFF *MY* TURF, AND I'LL STAY OFF *YOURS*" WAS ONE.

"MIND YOUR OWN *BUSINESS*" WAS ANOTHER.

THE ACTS OF VENGEANCE CHANGED ALL THAT.

WHEN YOU TRADE ENEMIES, YOU END UP TRADING TURF-- WHETHER YOU PLAN TO OR NOT.

SOME PEOPLE HAVEN'T TAKEN TO THAT VERY WELL.

WON-DERFUL. JUST WHAT I NEED TO BREAK MY DAY.

ANOTHER VILLAIN *FREE*-FOR-ALL....

...THIRD ONE THIS WEEK.

THIS TIME IT'S THE RHINO VERSUS SHOCKER AND HYDRO-MAN.

=OUUF!=

DON'T THESE PEOPLE HAVE SOAP OPERAS TO WATCH?

OWWW! SPIDER-SENSE BLARING-- WARNING-- DANGER--!

HEY!

WHAT'S THE IDEA?

WE SAW YOU WRECK THE *TRIBORO BRIDGE*--SAW IT ON THE *NEWS!*

YEAH! HEARD YOU ALMOST CAPSIZED THE *STATEN ISLAND FERRY,* TOO!

SUPER-POWERED *MANIAC!*

WAITASECOND, THAT'S NOT THE WAY IT HAPPENED--

YOU'RE A *MENACE!*

ALL YOU SUPER-CREEPS, WORSE THAN *MUTIES!*

GO HOME!

GET OUTTA HERE!

CREEP!

MANIAC!

MENACE!

WELL, WELL, WELL, WELL, WELL.

THEY SAY EVERY DOG HAS HIS DAY.

LOOKS LIKE *THIS* DAY IS YOURS, NICKIE KATZENBERG.

I KNOW A GUY WHO'S GONNA LOVE THIS PIC ALMOST AS MUCH AS *I* DO.

I CAN SEE THE HEADLINE NOW: "*SPIDER-MENACE PURSUED BY ANGRY MOB!*"

WOOF! BOW-WOW.

CLIK

AAAAROOOO!

MIDTOWN MANHATTAN.

SOMEWHERE NOT FAR FROM THE OFFICE TOWER OWNED BY WILSON FISK...

...a.k.a. *THE KINGPIN.*

"ALL SYSTEMS APPEAR *INTACT.*

"SURPRISINGLY, WHAT LITTLE CORROSION WAS CAUSED BY THE ARTIFACT'S IMMERSION IN *SEA WATER* THESE LAST FEW DAYS SEEMS *NEGLIGIBLE* AT WORST...

"MOREOVER, MY *MODIFICATIONS* TO THE ARTIFACT'S PRIMITIVE MICRO-PROCESSOR ARE NOW *COMPLETE.*

DOOM.

A WORD WITH YOU.

YES?

PROJECT POWER (PROGRESS REPORT): "FOR THE PAST SEVERAL HOURS MY MACHINES HAVE PROBED AND REPAIRED THE ARTIFACT DESIGNATED T.E.S.S. — *ONE.*

WE AGREED, ALL OF US, TO SHARE OUR RESOURCES WHEN WE EMBARKED ON THESE *ACTS OF VENGEANCE* AGAINST OUR MOST PERSISTENT FOES.

BY TRADING ENEMIES, WE HOPE TO WIN A LONG-DELAYED *VICTORY* OVER THE FORCES THAT OPPOSE US.

BUT FOR THIS PLAN TO SUCCEED, YOU EACH MUST FOCUS YOUR ENERGIES ON THE *COMMON GOAL.*

THIS YOU HAVE FAILED TO DO, DOCTOR.

FRANKLY, YOU SEEM *OBSESSED* WITH SPIDER-MAN'S PURPORTED "NEW POWERS"...

...AND I WONDER *WHY?*

135

IF I AM OBSESSED, IT IS WITH A DESIRE TO SEE THE WEB-SPINNER UTTERLY *DESTROYED.*

OBSERVE.

T.E.S.S.-ONE... STATE YOUR MISSION.

TOTAL ELIMINATION OF *SUPER-SOLDIERS.*

T.E.S.S.-ONE...IDENTIFY THE SUPER-POWERED BEING ON THE TELEVISOR MONITOR BEFORE YOU.

BEING IS SUPER-POWERED?

CORRECT.

IN FACT, BEING IS A *SUPER-SOLDIER.*

AND WHAT DOES YOUR PROGRAMMING REQUIRE YOU TO *DO* WHEN YOU ENCOUNTER A SUPER-SOLDIER, T.E.S.S.-*ONE?*

ELIMINATE!

KRASSH

SATISFACTORY.

BUT WHAT WILL PREVENT THIS MACHINE FROM TURNING AGAINST *US,* DOOM?

DON'T CONCERN YOURSELF WITH *IMPOSSIBILITIES,* KINGPIN.

THE ARTIFACT IS UNDER MY *COMPLETE* CONTROL.

AND THAT, DEAR DOCTOR, IS *PRECISELY* WHAT CONCERNS *ME.*

THE NEW *SOHO* LOFT APARTMENT OF PETER AND MARY JANE PARKER.

DARN. WISH PETER WERE HOME.

HANGING PICTURES ON YOUR OWN IS A ROYAL *PILL*--

THEN ALLOW ME.

EEE!

Oh.

IT'S YOU.

"OH, IT'S *YOU*"?

WHAT KIND OF WELCOME IS THAT?

PETER, WE'VE BEEN IN THIS APARTMENT *WEEKS* NOW-- BUT OTHER THAN THE TIME WE SPEND *ASLEEP*, WE HAVEN'T SPENT AN *HOUR* ALONE TOGETHER SINCE WE MOVED.

SO EXCUSE ME IF MY DARLING HUBBY SEEMS LIKE A *STRANGER*, OKAY?

SORRY, MJ.

LIFE'S BEEN *HECTIC* LATELY.

BECAUSE OF THESE *NEW* POWERS--

RIGHT.

DID YOU KNOW, PEOPLE ACTUALLY *HECKLED* ME IN TIMES SQUARE TODAY?

I SAVED THEIR *LIVES*-- AND THEY ACT LIKE *I* WAS THE MENACE!

PETER, I SAW THAT BATTLE ON THE *TV NEWS*.

YOU *WERE* A MENACE-- OR AT LEAST YOU *LOOKED* LIKE A MENACE.

FACE IT, YOUR NEW POWERS CAN BE PRETTY *OVER-WHELMING*-- EVEN AT A DISTANCE.

HUH?

I DON'T BELIEVE THIS! YOU SOUND AS IF YOU *AGREE* WITH THOSE ANTI-SUPER BEING *FANATICS*--

PETER, I NEVER SAID--

MY OWN *WIFE!* SIDING WITH CREEPS AND *PROTO-FACISTS!*

PETER, THIS IS RIDICU-LOUS! YOU AREN'T *LISTENING* TO--

WHAT'S TO *HEAR?*

I EXPECT SUPPORT-- *COMPASSION*-- BUT YOU'RE LIKE ALL THE REST!

I'M *OUTTA* HERE!

PETER?

MY GOD... WHAT'S *HAPPENING* TO HIM?

MY GOD... WHAT'S *HAPPENING* TO ME?

I LOVE THAT WOMAN-- AND I PRACTICALLY CHEWED HER HEAD OFF--FOR *WHAT?*

EVER SINCE I GOT THESE NEW POWERS, *ALL* MY REACTIONS HAVE BECOME HYPER-SENSITIVE!

MAYBE I BETTER GO HOME AND--

AAARRGH.!

TALK ABOUT *HYPER-REACTIONS!*

ALONG WITH EVERYTHING ELSE, MY *SPIDER-SENSE* IS SO POWERFUL NOW--

-- I'M PRACTICALLY *BLINDED* WITH PAIN EVERY TIME IT WARNS ME OF DANGER!

MAKES ME WONDER WHICH IS *WORSE*-- THE THREAT OR THE ALARM?

UH-OH...

THIS TIME... DEFINITELY THE *THREAT!*

TARGET DETECTED.

EXECUTING PRIMARY PROGRAM DIRECTIVES:

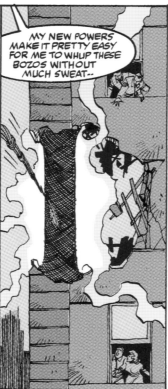

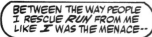

BETWEEN THE WAY PEOPLE I RESCUE *RUN* FROM ME LIKE *I* WAS THE MENACE--

-- AND THE WAY THESE WOODWORK-CRAWLERS KEEP *ATTACKING* ME--

--MY PERSECUTION COMPLEX IS GETTING A REAL *WORKOUT*-- eh?

OH, PLEASE GIVE ME A BREAK.

AND *ANOTHER* THING:

THWIPP

SEVERAL TIMES WHEN I'VE USED MY POWERS THE LAST FEW DAYS, I'VE HAD THE WEIRD *FEELING* THERE'S ANOTHER *PRESENCE* INSIDE ME!

"AS IF SOMEONE WERE *WHISPERING* IN MY EAR--

"-- I CAN HEAR A *VOICE*... BUT I CAN'T *MAKE OUT* WHAT THE VOICE IS *SAYING!*"

YOU WEB-SLINGING LUNATIC!

WHAT *RIGHT* DO YOU HAVE TO TURN *OUR* STREETS INTO A BATTLEFIELD?

≥SIGH≤

THAT VOICE I CAN HEAR.

YEAH! THIS CITY WOULDN'T HAVE ANY TROUBLE IF IT WASN'T FOR CREEPS LIKE YOU!

JUDGING BY THE *LOOK* THOSE PEOPLE GAVE ME--

--ANY *GAINS* THOMAS FIREHEART'S PRO-SPIDEY P.R. CAMPAIGN MAY HAVE MADE FOR ME THESE LAST FEW WEEKS-- --JUST WENT *SMASH* INTO THE QUEENSBORO BRIDGE ALONG WITH THAT ROBOT.

FRANKLY, I COULDN'T CARE *LESS.*

THE WHOLE HUMAN RACE CAN GO SKINNY-DIP IN A *CESS POOL* FOR ALL I--*huh?*

WHAT AM I *SEEING?*

IS THAT ROBOT REALLY *ABSORBING* THE BRIDGE SUPERSTRUCTURE TO REPAIR ITSELF?

OR HAVE I FINALLY GONE OVER THE EDGE INTO *WEBBY WONDER LAND?*

PROJECT POWER (PROGRESS REPORT): "AS PROGRAMMED, T.E.S.S.-*ONE* IS RESPONDING TO THE MODIFICATIONS IN ITS DESIGN IMPLEMENTED BY MY EQUIPMENT.

"THE ROBOT IS NOW CAPABLE OF *ABSORBING* ANY MATERIALS OR ENERGIES IT REQUIRES TO FULFILL ITS MISSION.

"ULTIMATELY, IN ITS EFFORTS TO DESTROY ITS TARGET, THE ARTIFACT WILL BE FORCED TO DRAW ON THE WEB-SPINNER'S *OWN ENERGIES* TO DEFEAT HIM.

"ONCE THOSE ENERGIES HAVE BEEN ASSIMILATED BY T.E.S.S.-ONE.....

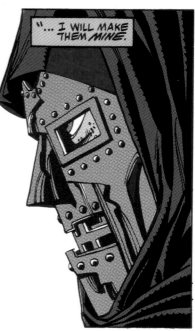

"... I WILL MAKE THEM *MINE.*

WONDERFUL. NOW I NEED A NEW PAIR OF *GLOVES.*

UH-OH.

LISTEN--ABOUT THAT *MENACE* CRACK--

--I WAS ONLY *KIDDING!*

... I WAS ONLY *KIDDING...*

EPILOGUE: PROJECT POWER (PROGRESS REPORT): "EVENTS HAVE OUT-PACED EXPECTATIONS.

WHAT A LOUSY BREAK, EH?

WE JUST FINISH REFURBISHING THE BRIDGE UPPER ROADWAY--

-- AND NOW SOME JERK SUPER HERO WRECKS IT AGAIN!

"RETRIEVING THE ARTIFACT THIS TIME IS SIMPLICITY ITSELF.

"A HOMING DEVICE IN THE MODIFIED SKULL-CASING LEADS ME AT ONCE TO MY TARGET.

"TELEMETRY READ-OUTS CONFIRM MY CALCULATIONS.

"THE ARTIFACT HAS ABSORBED A QUANTITY OF THE ENERGIES SPIDER-MAN EXPENDED DURING THE CLIMACTIC STAGE OF BATTLE.

"INSUFFICIENT TO ALLOW T.E.S.S.-ONE THE OPTION TO RE-CONSTRUCT ITSELF, PERHAPS--

"--BUT MORE THAN ADEQUATE FOR MY NEEDS, I THINK.

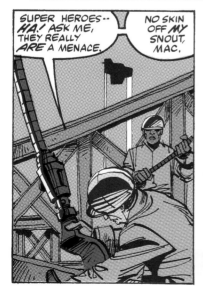

SUPER HEROES-- HA! ASK ME, THEY REALLY ARE A MENACE.

NO SKIN OFF MY SNOUT, MAC.

ME, I LIKE OVERTIME PAY.

PROJECT POWER (REPORT, CONTINUED): "WITH THE POWER STORED IN THE ARTIFACT'S SKULL-CASING, I WILL SOON ACHIEVE MY DESTINY.

"FOR POWER IS DESTINY...

"...AND DESTINY IS DOOM."

CHAPTER 8

IT'S A **FAKE**.

AN **OBVIOUS** FRAUD.

SINCE WE BEGAN THESE **ACTS OF VENGEANCE** -- TRADING ENEMIES TO GAIN ADVANTAGE OVER OUR LONG-TIME FOES --

-- SPIDER-MAN HAS REMAINED THE **ONE** HERO WHO CONSISTENTLY DEFIED OUR ATTEMPTS AT HIS **DESTRUCTION**.

PRECISELY. WHY SHOULD HE **RESIGN** THE GAME NOW?

IT MAKES NO SENSE, **WIZARD**.

I CAN ONLY REPORT WHAT I WITNESSED, KINGPIN.

EVEN AT A DISTANCE, THROUGH A STORM, I HEARD HIM BABBLE SOMETHING ABOUT "TOO MUCH RESPONSIBILITY" --

BAH.

HE CAN'T QUIT.

I WON'T **ALLOW** HIM TO QUIT.

NOR WILL I -- AND THIS MASK WILL HELP US **FIND** HIM, AND ULTIMATELY, **DESTROY** HIM.

EH? THAT MASK?

WHAT ARE YOU GOING TO DO, FOOL -- TRACK THE WEB-SLINGER WITH A **BLOOD-HOUND**?

THIS IS ABSURD.

WASTE TIME WITH **JESTS** IF YOU LIKE, MAGNETO. **DOOM**, FOR ONE, HAS NO **PATIENCE** FOR THIS DRIVEL.

WHEN YOU'RE READY TO TAKE ACTION ON A SCALE BEFITTING OUR COMBINED RESOURCES, *SUMMON* ME.

UNTIL THEN, DO AS YOU WILL -- BUT WITHOUT *ME.*

I HAVE A CRITICAL PROJECT NEARING *COMPLETION* IN MY LAB.

WHAT *SORT* OF PROJECT, DOCTOR DOOM?

AND HOW, I WONDER, WILL IT AFFECT *MY* PLANS...?

A *BLOODHOUND,* MAGNETO?

YOU'RE *NOT FAR OFF.*

GENTLEMEN, IN MY CAPACITY AS LEADER OF *THE FRIGHTFUL FOUR* --

-- I'VE WORKED WITH *MANY* PARTNERS.

EACH WAS A *WORTHY* WARRIOR IN HIS OR HER OWN RIGHT.

BUT *NONE,* I THINK YOU'LL AGREE, IS AS *PHYSICALLY INTIMIDATING* AS THIS, OUR MOST RECENT ADDITION --

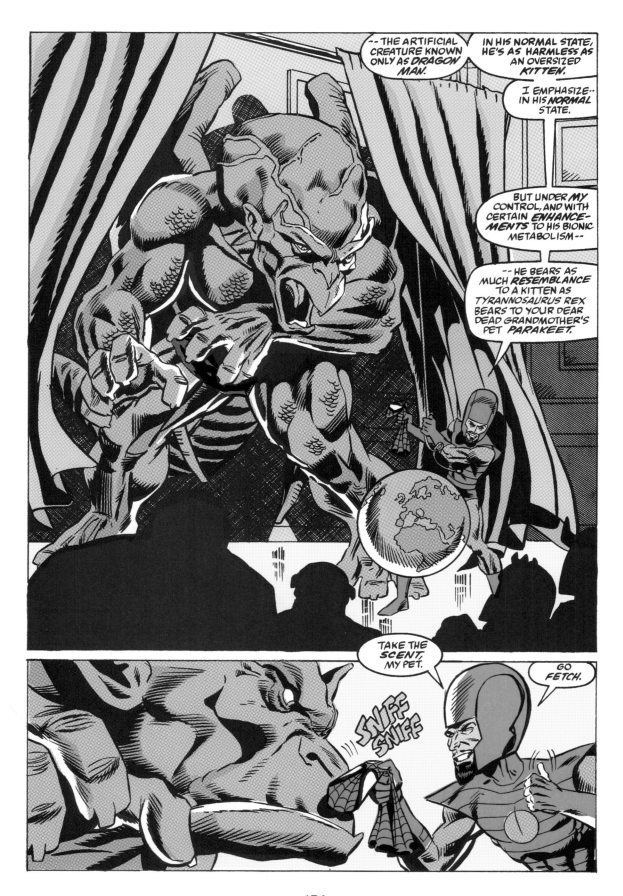

ONCE UPON A TIME, THERE WERE DRAGONS IN THE LAND...

GREAT WINGED BEASTS WHO BREATHED *FIRE* AND ATE *MAIDENS* AND DIED ON THE LANCES OF MIGHTY ARMORED *HEROES.*

SNIFF SNIFF

SNIFF SNIFF?

SNIFF!?

SNIFF SNIFF? SNORT

SNIFF SNIFF SNIFF

ONCE UPON A TIME...

SPRING STREET STATION, I.R.T. UPTOWN.

I DIDN'T *ASK* FOR THESE POWERS.

IF I CAN'T HANDLE THEM, THAT ISN'T *MY* FAULT.

ALL I WANT IS A *LIFE* LIKE ANYONE ELSE.

RIDE THE SUBWAY, GO TO SCHOOL, LOVE MY WIFE, BABYSIT A KID...

FAWHOOM

INTERLUDE: THE LAB OF *VICTOR VON DOOM*, ONCE, AND FUTURE MONARCH OF *LATVERIA*.

RECORDING: PROJECT POWER, PROGRESS REPORT. MY PLAN TO SIPHON A PORTION OF *SPIDER-MAN'S* NEW-FOUND *COSMIC ENERGY* BY MEANS OF THE ROBOT, *T.E.S.S.-ONE*--

--SEEMS TO 'HAVE *SUCCEEDED* BEYOND MY *EXPECTATIONS.*

SOON, A SHARE OF THAT POWER WILL BE *MINE.*

THEN I WILL HAVE NO NEED OF *ALLIES* TO COMPLETE MY PERSONAL *ACT OF VENGEANCE.*

THEN SHALL *DOOM* ACHIEVE HIS *DESTINY..*

UNFORTUNATE-- BUT HARDLY A *SURPRISE.*

OF THE *CORE GROUP*, DOCTOR DOOM WAS THE ONE I FELT LEAST ABLE TO *MANIPULATE.*

HIS WILL IS ALMOST THE EQUAL OF *MINE.*

I DO HOPE I WON'T HAVE TO *DESTROY* HIM...

DRAGON MAN IS SO BUSY POUNDING THE FRONT CAR OF THIS TRAIN--LIKE A REFUGEE FROM *SKULL ISLAND*--

--HE DOESN'T REALIZE I PROTECTED EVERYBODY INSIDE WITH AIR-BAG STYLE *WEB-PILLOWS* BEFORE HIS FIRST PUNCH EVEN *CONNECTED.*

NOT ONLY DOES DRAGON MAN HAVE THE *PERSONALITY* OF A PILEDRIVER, HE'S GOT THE BRAINS TO MATCH.

SNIFF

AH, HERE COME THE HAPPY *PASSENGERS.*

WHAT *ELSE* SHOULD I EXPECT FROM--

NO!

W-WHAT *IS* IT--
A *GAS MAIN*
EXPLOSION?

NO! IT'S
*SPIDER-
MAN!*

OH, YEAH,
RIGHT.-
BLAME IT
ON ME.

IGNORE THE BIG GRAY BEASTIE,
NEVER MIND I JUST SAVED A
TRAINLOAD OF COMMUTERS.

NONE OF IT WOULD'VE
HAPPENED IF I HADN'T
BEEN AROUND, RIGHT?

ISN'T THAT WHAT
YOU'RE *THINKING?*

WELL, DON'T
WORRY.

ONCE I DROP THIS BOZO AT
THE VAULT, I'M OUTTA THE
SUPER HERO BIZ *PERMANENTLY.*

IF I WANTED ABUSE LIKE THIS, I'D GET A JOB TEACHING *HIGH SCHOOL.*

THERE HE IS!

DON'T LET HIM GET AWAY!

YEAH! I WANNA *THANK* THE GUY!

IF IT WEREN'T FOR SPIDER-MAN, WE'D BE *DEAD!*

SPIDEY! CAN I HAVE YOUR *AUTOGRAPH?*

SAVE ONE FOR ME!

YOU'RE KIDDING!

THE WAY YOU STOOD UP TO THAT *MONSTER* --

-- I DON'T CARE WHAT *ANYONE* SAYS, YOU'RE A *HERO* IN MY BOOK!

ONCE UPON A TIME, HE THOUGHT *POWER* WOULD MAKE HIM HAPPY.

ONCE UPON A TIME, HE THOUGHT *POWER* WOULD SOLVE HIS PROBLEMS...

ALL RIGHT, NEW YORK!

...ALL AT ONCE, FOREVER AND EVER.

NOW, IN HIS *HEART,* HE KNOWS IT CAN'T.

BUT JUST FOR A LITTLE WHILE, HE'S WILLING TO PRETEND IT *CAN.*

ONCE UPON A TIME...

OH, NO. I HOPED TO *FINISH* SPIDER-MAN WITH THIS ATTACK!

INSTEAD, I BROUGHT HIM BACK TO THE GAME AS AN *EAGER* PLAYER!

GASP! WHEN THE *OTHERS* FIND OUT --

"-- THEIR NEXT *ACT OF VENGEANCE* --

-- MAY BE AGAINST *ME!*"

CHAPTER 9

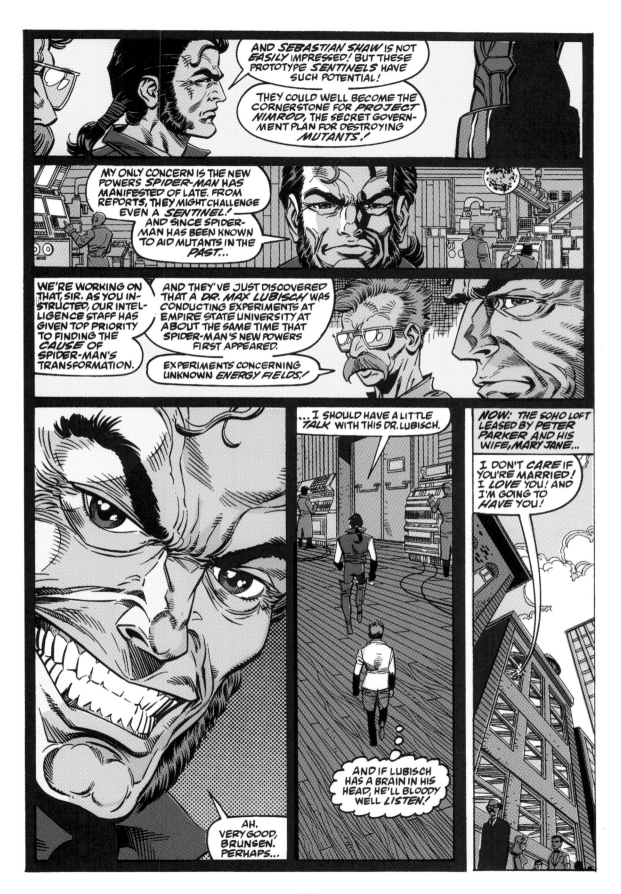

AND *SEBASTIAN SHAW* IS NOT *EASILY* IMPRESSED! BUT THESE PROTOTYPE *SENTINELS* HAVE SUCH POTENTIAL!

THEY COULD WELL BECOME THE CORNERSTONE FOR *PROJECT NIMROD*, THE SECRET GOVERNMENT PLAN FOR DESTROYING *MUTANTS!*

MY ONLY CONCERN IS THE NEW POWERS *SPIDER-MAN* HAS MANIFESTED OF LATE. FROM REPORTS, THEY MIGHT CHALLENGE EVEN A *SENTINEL!* AND SINCE SPIDER-MAN HAS BEEN KNOWN TO AID MUTANTS IN THE *PAST...*

WE'RE WORKING ON THAT, SIR. AS YOU INSTRUCTED, OUR INTELLIGENCE STAFF HAS GIVEN TOP PRIORITY TO FINDING THE *CAUSE* OF SPIDER-MAN'S TRANSFORMATION.

AND THEY'VE JUST DISCOVERED THAT A *DR. MAX LUBISCH* WAS CONDUCTING EXPERIMENTS AT EMPIRE STATE UNIVERSITY AT ABOUT THE SAME TIME THAT SPIDER-MAN'S NEW POWERS FIRST APPEARED.

EXPERIMENTS CONCERNING UNKNOWN *ENERGY FIELDS!*

...I SHOULD HAVE A LITTLE *TALK* WITH THIS DR. LUBISCH.

NOW: THE SOHO LOFT LEASED BY PETER PARKER AND HIS WIFE, MARY JANE...

I DON'T *CARE* IF YOU'RE MARRIED! I *LOVE* YOU! AND I'M GOING TO *HAVE* YOU!

AND IF LUBISCH HAS A BRAIN IN HIS HEAD, HE'LL BLOODY WELL *LISTEN!*

AH. VERY GOOD, BRUNSEN. PERHAPS...

I KNOW YOU'RE USED TO GETTING WHAT YOU WANT, SYBIL, BUT THIS TIME YOU'RE NOT GOING TO WINE! I- I MEAN, WIN!

GUESS IT'S OBVIOUS WHO THE REAL ACTOR IN THIS FAMILY IS!

HEY, HON, NO PROBLEM!

AW, DARN IT, MJ! I'M SORRY.

YOUR HELPING ME LEARN LINES FOR MY PART IN "SECRET HOSPITAL" IS A HUGE HELP! REALLY!

WE JUST NEED A BREAK, THAT'S ALL.

I DOUBT IT'LL HELP.

I CAN'T SEEM TO CONCENTRATE ON ANYTHING SINCE MY SPIDER-MAN POWERS WENT SCREWY!

MY GRADUATE STUDIES HAVE SUFFERED, MY SOCIAL LIFE IS NIL.

I CAN'T STOP WONDERING HOW I GOT THESE NEW ABILITIES.

OR MORE IMPORTANTLY, WHY!

YOU KNOW, TAKING A LITTLE SPIN ALWAYS HELPED CLEAR YOUR HEAD BEFORE.

BUT THERE'S NO GUARANTEE THAT TRAINING THIS MECHANISM ON *SPIDER-MAN* WILL NEGATE HIS NEW POWERS!

CONFOUND IT! I'M SICK OF THIS BULLYING! DON'T KNOW WHY I LET YOU ORDER ME AROUND IN THE *FIRST* PLACE!

NO? COULD IT BE THAT *ODD RUMOR* MY RESEARCH STAFF UNEARTHED? ABOUT THE RATHER UNORTH-ODOX *EXPERIMENT* THAT COST YOU YOUR POISITION IN HEIDELBERG?

MESSY BUSINESS, THAT.

Y-YES...

-gulp-

Y-YES, IT WOULD.

THERE'S NO PROOF THAT MY EX-PERIMENTS ARE EVEN *REMOTELY* LINKED TO SPIDER-MAN AT ALL!

WE'LL NEVER KNOW UNTIL WE *TRY*, eh, DOCTOR?

BE A PITY IF THE UNIVERSITY'S *BOARD OF DIRECTORS* WERE TO HEAR OF IT...HMMM?

I'M GLAD WE UNDERSTAND EACH OTHER, DOCTOR.

CARRY ON.

WHA--? THE SENTINELS! TH-THEY'RE *MOVING*!

THAT'S *IMPOSSIBLE*!

THEIR *POWER* ISN'T *ON*!

HEADING STRAIGHT FOR EACH OTHER! STARTING TO *GLOW*! THEY--

FASH

SYSTEMS CHECK COMPLETED. UNIT ON-LINE AND FUNCTIONING.

REPROGRAMMED PRIME DIRECTIVE OPERATIONAL.

THEY'VE *MERGED*! F-FORMED SOME SORT OF *TRI-SENTINEL*!

WE'RE *DOOMED*!

SPA-

KASH

WE'RE *NOT* DOOMED?

THAT FLASH OF LIGHT--?

YES! *THERE*!

KEEP HIM IN SIGHT, CARLSON! GET CLOSE!

LUBISCH! PREPARE THE *ENERGY PROJECTOR*!

UUUUUUUHH, PERHAPS... I-IN THE FUTURE... I SHOULD CONCERN MYSELF WITH LESS *FORMIDABLE* OPPONENTS! L-LIKE...

...GALACTUS?

EEEYAAAHH!

SPIDER-SENSE! L-LIKE A *BUZZ SAW*! R-RIPPING MY HEAD APART!

SO STRONG, C-CAN'T EVEN TELL WHERE THE DANGER'S *COMING FROM*!

NOW, LUBISCH!

ACTIVATE THE PROJECTOR... *NOW*!

S-SOMETHING'S HAPPENING!

I'M CHANGING!

I'M *REMEMBERING!*

I'M--

175

SPIDER-SENSE RAGING! WARNING ME TO *GET AWAY!*

HAVE TO HOLD OFF, IGNORE MY INSTINCTS UNTIL I FINISH REPAIRS! EVEN IF THAT MEANS GETTING--

--CAUGHT?

WAIT! THAT THING SPIDER-MAN IS *FIGHTING!* IT...I-IT LOOKS LIKE--

--OH, MY DEAR LORD...!

BRUNSEN! TELL ME THE SENTINELS ARE STILL WITH YOU IN THE LAB!

WELL, ACTUALLY, MR. SHAW, WE'VE HAD A LITTLE PROBLEM--

YOU'RE FIRED!

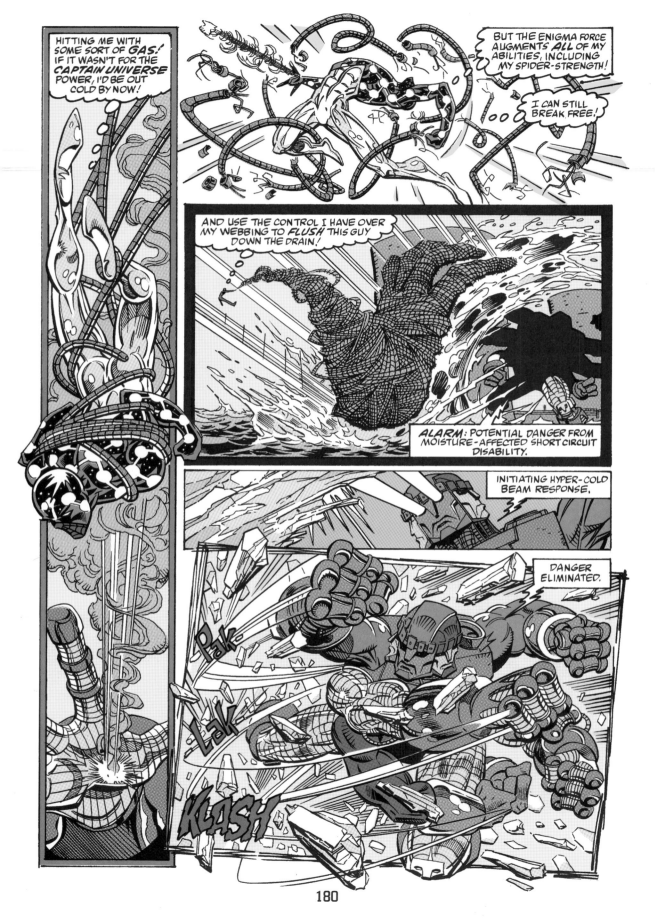

HITTING ME WITH SOME SORT OF *GAS!* IF IT WASN'T FOR THE *CAPTAIN UNIVERSE* POWER, I'D BE OUT COLD BY NOW!

BUT THE ENIGMA FORCE AUGMENTS *ALL* OF MY ABILITIES, INCLUDING MY SPIDER-STRENGTH!

I CAN STILL BREAK FREE!

AND USE THE CONTROL I HAVE OVER MY WEBBING TO *FLUSH* THIS GUY DOWN THE DRAIN.!

ALARM: POTENTIAL DANGER FROM MOISTURE-AFFECTED SHORT CIRCUIT DISABILITY.

INITIATING HYPER-COLD BEAM RESPONSE.

DANGER ELIMINATED.

Pak

Lak

KLASH

NO CHOICE! GOT TO DO THIS ONE-ON-ONE! START RIPPING HIS GUTS OUT--

-- AND HOPE THAT *STOPS* HIM BEFORE HE *RETURNS* THE FAVOR!

IMPEDING ANNOYANCE REMOVED.

≥ whrnk ?! ≤

LOKI-COMMANDED PRIME DIRECTIVE NEARING FULFILLMENT.

NUCLEAR DEVASTATION: *IMMINENT.*

BLAST! I WAS HOPING I WOULDN'T HAVE TO DO THIS...!

PUK

WHA--?! I--IT STOPPED!

STOPPED COLD!

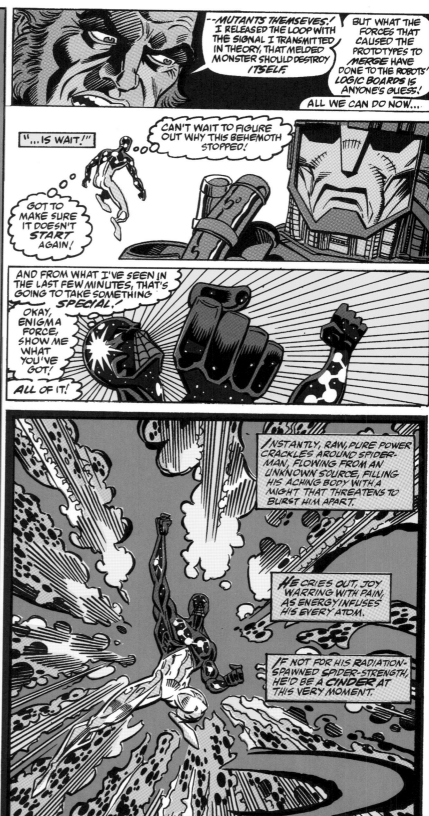

IN A MOMENT MORE, HE MAY BE ONE ANY-WAY!

IT'S MOVING AGAIN! SWINGING ON THE CONTAINMENT TOWER!

TRIPLED LOGIC CAPACITY MUST HAVE BEEN ABLE TO *REJECT* THE FAIL-SAFE LOOP!

GENTLEMEN... WE ARE ABOUT TO DIE.

NO.

YOU'RE NOT.

THANKS TO THE IRON WILL OF THE AMAZING SPIDER-MAN.

AND TO THE UNCATEGORIZABLE POWER OF CAPTAIN UNIVERSE!

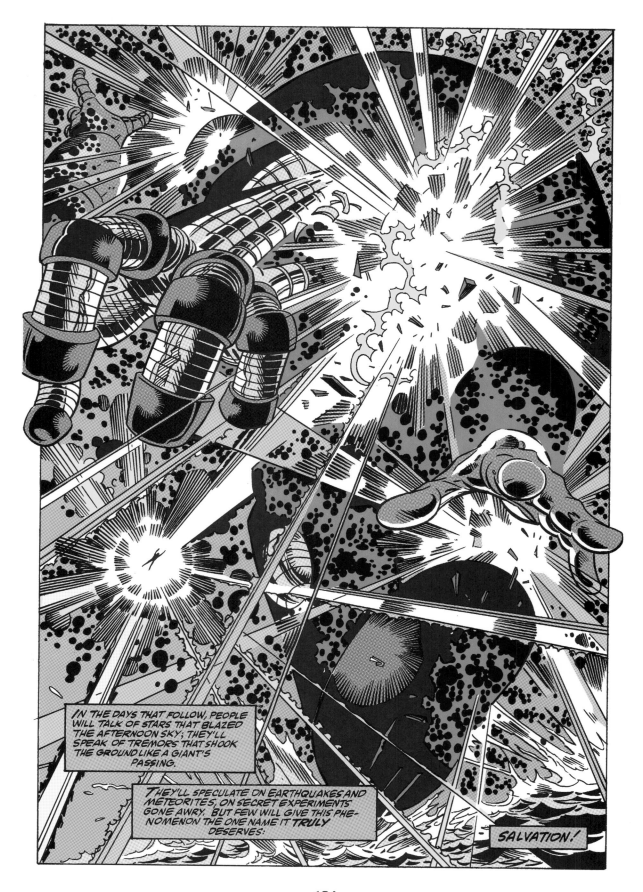

IN THE DAYS THAT FOLLOW, PEOPLE WILL TALK OF STARS THAT BLAZED THE AFTERNOON SKY; THEY'LL SPEAK OF TREMORS THAT SHOOK THE GROUND LIKE A GIANT'S PASSING.

THEY'LL SPECULATE ON EARTHQUAKES AND METEORITES, ON SECRET EXPERIMENTS GONE AWRY. BUT FEW WILL GIVE THIS PHE-NOMENON THE ONE NAME IT *TRULY* DESERVES:

SALVATION!

I'M IMPRESSED.

THE ROBOT DISINTEGRATED, RENDERED TO *DUST!* RAMIFICATIONS COULD AFFECT *PROJECT NIMROD.* BUT, FOR NOW...

CARLSON? DROP DR. LUBISCH OFF AT *E.S.U.* THEN TAKE US HOME. AND WHILE YOU'RE AT IT--

--GET MY *INSURANCE* PEOPLE ON THE PHONE, WOULD YOU?

UUHHHHHHH.

FEEL...DIFFERENT. I MEAN... *BESIDES* FEELING...HALF DEAD!

COSTUME'S... CHANGED BACK. BUT...HAVE I? I-I'LL TRY...

⩾HNF!⩽ NOPE. C-CAN'T FLY... NOT AN INCH!

I'M BACK...TO *NORMAL!*

WELL...SORT OF! SO ZONKED...

THWIPP

...CAN'T EVEN SHOOT MY *WEBBING*...STRAIGHT!

SHOULD GO HOME... BUT MAYBE...I'LL JUST REST...A MINUTE...

...A WEEK...

...A YEA...⁂

*S*IRENS SOON WAKE THE SLUMBERING HERO. HE HOBBLES AND HITCHES, EVENTUALLY WEB-SWINGING HIS WAY BACK TO MANHATTAN.

*W*HERE EVENTUALLY, TIME-- ALONG WITH A LOVING WIFE AND SUPER-HUMAN RECUPERATIVE ABILITIES-- HEAL HIS MASSIVE EXHAUSTION.

I CAN'T HELP THINKING I SHOULD HAVE DONE *MORE,* MARY JANE.

I MEAN, WITH ALL THAT POWER, I COULD HAVE STOPPED *KHADAFI!* ENDED *APARTHEID!*

SOMETHING!

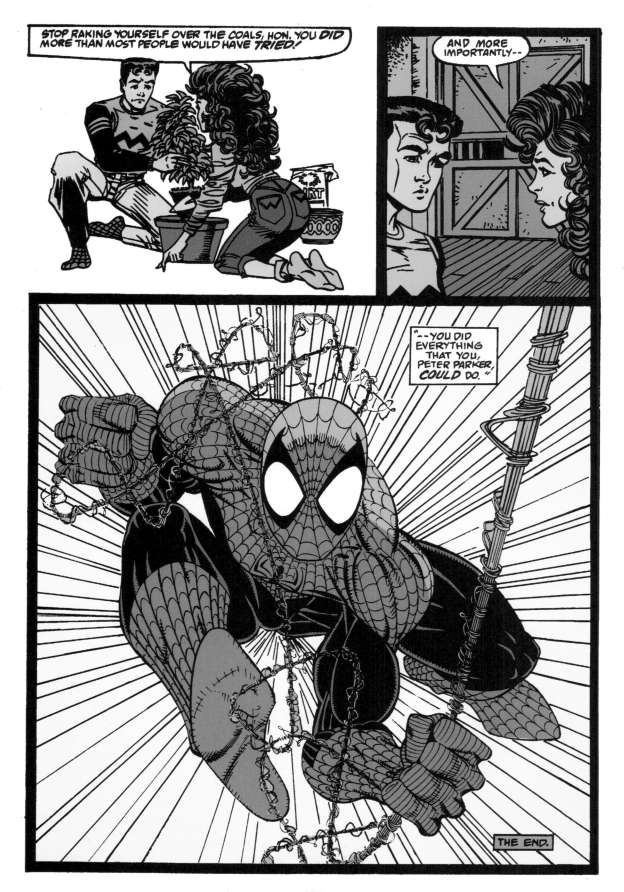

STOP RAKING YOURSELF OVER THE COALS, HON. YOU *DID* MORE THAN MOST PEOPLE WOULD HAVE *TRIED!*

AND MORE IMPORTANTLY--

"--YOU DID EVERYTHING THAT YOU, PETER PARKER, *COULD DO.*"

THE END.

"...MUST COME GREATER RESPONSIBILITY"

by Peter Sanderson

Some loose ends to tie up...

As you have by now realized, the mysterious stranger behind the "Acts of Vengeance" conspiracy was Loki, the Asgardian god of evil and arch-enemy of his foster brother, Thor. But Loki has no quarrel with Spider-Man, so why, you might ask, would he instigate attacks against him? It is true that Loki is also the god of mischief, and enjoys stirring up destructive chaos for its own sake. But Spider-Man was not Loki's real target. Years ago, Loki attempted to manipulate Thor into battling the Hulk, whom Loki hoped would crush him. But the scheme backfired when Thor formed an alliance with the Hulk, Iron Man , the original Ant-Man, and the Wasp, creating the Avengers. It was a constant irritation to Loki that he had brought about the team's creation. So Loki brought about the"Acts of Vengeance" to destroy the Avengers. It mattered little to him if his villainous pawns killed other super heroes, including Spider-Man, in the process. (Ironically, Spider-Man had twice come close to joining the Avengers, and finally became a reserve member shortly after the "Acts.")

Virtually every one of the villains involved with the Acts eventually paid a heavy price for his misdeeds. Loki was finally revealed to be the mastermind behind the conspiracy and was defeated in combat by Thor. The "Gang of Six" who coordinated the "Acts" fell apart, each one getting the comeuppance he so justly deserved. It should be noted that Doctor Doom had no part in the "Acts" debacle. The Doom who served in the conspiracy was only one of Doctor Doom's numerous robots, programmed to behave like the real Doom and pursue his interests in his absence.

As for Titania, the Trapster, and the Brothers Grimm, they were being taken to the Vault when they were rescued by Graviton. Spidey's longtime enemy, Chameleon, then sent all of them and Goliath to attack Spider-Man again. Spider-Man, minus his cosmic powers, still managed to defeat his foes, relying on his strength, speed, agility, and wits.

Marvel readers first learned about the "Uni-Power " that gave Spider-Man his cosmic powers in the 1970s and early 1980s. We have seen a number of "Captain Universes" over the years, ranging from a baby to the sorcerer Doctor Strange and The Hulk's alter ego, Bruce Banner. It is said that at all times there is a Captain Universe somewhere on Earth. The origin of the Uni-Power is as yet unknown.

Finally, Thomas Fireheart tired of owning the Daily Bugle and sold it back to J. Jonah Jameson for merely a dollar. So Spider-Man is once again back to his "normal" level of super power and Jameson is back writing Bugle editorials against him. And that's just about as happy an ending as your ever-beleaguered friendly neighborhood Spider-Man can expect!

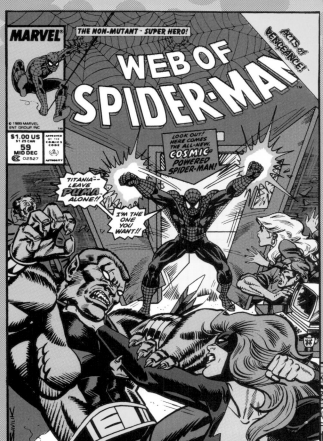